THE MAN WHO SOLD PRAYERS

Books now available in the International Fiction List

JOSEF SKVORECKY *The Bass Saxophone*
MARIE-CLAIRE BLAIS *Deaf to the City*
JOY KOGAWA *Obasan*
ITALO CALVINO *If on a winter's night a traveller*
MARGARET CREAL *The Man Who Sold Prayers*
JAROSLAV HASEK *The Red Commissar*
Authors shortly to be published in the International Fiction List
include: *Manuel Mujica Lainez, Barry Callaghan, James
Kennaway, Jorge Luis Borges, H.R. Percy.*

THE INTERNATIONAL FICTION LIST

It is our intention, with the International Fiction List, to seek out and publish fine fiction — new works as well as classics — by authors from around the world. This on-going series will, we hope, testify that good, and even great, fiction is still being written and is exciting, relevant and, above all else, wonderful to read.

The Editors

THE INTERNATIONAL FICTION LIST

THE MAN WHO SOLD PRAYERS

PRAYERS

Margaret Creal

LESTER
&ORPEN
DENNYS
PUBLISHERS

Canadian Cataloguing in Publication Data

Creal, Margaret.
    The man who sold prayers

ISBN 0-919630-18-9

I. Title.

PS3553.R42M36   813'.54   C81-094434-0

Jacket design by N.R. Jackson
Series design by Paul Hodgson for Fifty Fingers
Production by Paula Chabanais Productions
Typesetting by Trigraph
Set in 14 pt. Perpetua

Printed and bound in Canada by The Hunter Rose Company
Limited for
Lester & Orpen Dennys Limited
78 Sullivan Street
Toronto, Ontario
M5T 1C1

For Stephen, and for Catriona

CONTENTS

The man who sold prayers

SHORTLY AFTER HIS FORTY-FIFTH BIRTHDAY, THE REVEREND St. Clair Gwynn — known to his friends as Saintly — ceased to believe in God. Granted, it was not remarkable that in the mid-sixties of this troubled century a man's Belief should fail him; it was remarkable that it should have survived intact until then. From his earliest childhood it had not wavered, fight it as he might in his college years when first exposed to the liberating delights of other creeds — Atheism, Agnosticism, Communism, Despair, Who Cares? Saintly found then that Belief was as firmly fixed in his character as was the language he spoke. Indeed, it was very much part of the language he spoke. Son of a clergyman — a good man whom Saintly, to his discomfiture, had not loved — he had been nurtured on the King James Bible and the Book of Common Prayer. Cranmer's rich rhetoric was as familiar to him as the rhymes and verses his Hebridean mother recited to him, and the songs she sang as he was falling asleep, about a fisher-king, an exiled prince being sped across the sea in a bonny boat, a tender queen in a prison cage. These songs remained vivid in his memory and were recalled to him many years later when he became acquainted with the paintings of Max Beckmann. He was often astonished at the inexhaustibleness of such connections, and saw that all human lives and ages were bound together, all contained in the Divine memory. (His own memory he thought of as a chain on which every moment of his lifetime was hung, quietly pulsing, awaiting its moment of recollection.)

When he was very young, a line from Genesis I had taken his fancy. "He made the stars also." The casual extravagance of the act had pleased the eight-year-old Saintly, reminding him of the itinerant magician who had recently visited his Saskatchewan town, drawing rabbits from hats and a gold watch from the vest pocket of the school principal, a dour man with a slight squint in the left eye. Finally, from his outstretched empty hands the magician had flung a shower of golden coins. The coins had proved to be fake. Still, Saintly had pictured a similar gesture on the part of the Almighty, handfuls of stars being scattered across the floor of the sky. To the young Saintly the sky had been a pleasure dome of cloudscapes, shooting stars, miraculous dawns and apocalyptical sunsets, white lightning, northern lights in season, and mirages — grain elevators hovering with insouciant ease above the horizon while below them the (ordinarily) flat prairie rolled on shimmering waves of heat. Sometimes, when on a frosty night he had stood gazing into the starry sky, he had seemed to feel the prairie tipping beneath his feet as the planet earth spun softly on her appointed course.

There was no particular event in the year 1965 to shake his lifelong belief. He read, with professional and personal interest, books about the Death of God, and attended lectures on the subject. Appreciating that for many people it was useful, even necessary, to come to terms with this new theological happening, he continued to prefer for himself the living paradox of God's existence to the verbal paradox of His death. As far as he was concerned God was, is, and evermore shall be, presumably outlasting the stars and the sky in which they sparkled.

True, the sky was not the delight that once it had been. It was often obscured by smog, and stabbed by television antennae and the high-rise buildings of the Eastern Canadian city in which he lived. Things less celestial than stars and planets travelled across it now: planes, and rockets, space-ships, possibly flying saucers.

Far below, Saintly and his soul jogged along.

Saintly was rector of an average-sized parish in an average income suburb, loved by many and esteemed by all his parishioners. The usual things happened in his parish — infants were born, and growing up were by turns happy or unhappy, learned or failed to learn, fell in and out of love, bought cars and houses, met with accident, failure, disappointment, occasionally with some small success, took sick, died. Saintly, attentive to all these events, saw in each a microcosmic drama.

The church, dedicated to St. Jude, was a new building in contemporary style, erected and paid for during his incumbency. Sunday services were well-attended, and the parish house was a regular beehive of activity. Every evening there were meetings and discussion groups, there were monthly square dances, and annual bazaars and rummage sales, frequent productions of Gilbert and Sullivan as well as cynical plays by avant-garde young Canadian dramatists. There were religious instruction classes for children, and dancing classes, Corners for Brownies and Dens for Cub Scouts, there was a weekly Yoga class, and a weekly lunch party followed by card games for the Golden Age Group. Also, potluck suppers for Young Marrieds, and Circles for sewing. Documentary films were shown, and educational films about Buddhism, the tribal life of the Tsimshians in British Columbia, and other such subjects. In short, it was a lively parish, and Saintly, as his fond parishioners said, was always "on the go."

It was in autumn, just when all these enterprises were going into full crescendo, that Saintly admitted to himself that something was awry. He had come back from a month's vacation with his wife and children feeling as if he had had no vacation at all. The family doctor tested him for a variety of ailments and could find nothing organically amiss. A simple case of overwork, he told Saintly, and prescribed vitamin B and a day off each week. Compliant, Saintly took Mondays off. He played golf on fine days, and tried to look forward to the ice-skating season, his favourite. (He had been, in his youth, a hockey player of exceptional brilliance.) Sometimes he and his wife Ann went to a film or dined at an Italian restaurant. But he could not shake off the oppressive fatigue, and wakened each morning with a murky-mauve feeling about the day ahead. He thought of the colour as F double-flat, and had always associated it with the cry of the lake loon, whose night yodellings had often startled him out of childhood sleep, apprising him of loneliness, madness, and death. There was no pleasure for him in his life or his work. Boredom settled on him like dust.

His daughters, Emily and Camilla, complained that he didn't laugh any more, or tell them stories about his

childhood which by comparison with theirs was delight-
fully antediluvian. Fire engines pulled by horses! Wooden
sidewalks! Pigtailed Indians in buckboard wagons driving
down the main street! School dismissed early so the
children could go outside to watch an airplane fly over the
town! (From the open cockpit the pilot, eerie in cap and
goggles, had waved at the gaping crowd in the schoolyard,
and flown off into the pearly sky, trailing behind him a
colourful pennant on which was printed INDIAN HEAD
CHATAUQUA.)

Saintly roused himself. "Why don't you tell *me* a
story?"

Camilla told him a shaggy-dog story, and he laughed.
But they were not fooled; it was not a genuine laugh.

Soon he was beset by something more alarming than
fatigue. When celebrating the Eucharist at weekday and
Sunday services, he found himself unaccountably short of
breath. He could scarcely speak, and felt as if he had been
running a long hard race. Curiously, it only happened
when he was praying, never when he was preaching or
reading the Lessons for the day, or the Epistle and Gospel.
Ann was surprised to hear about it. She said he sounded
"perfectly normal". He decided it must be his imagination,
and considered going to the Yoga class to learn how to
breathe. But the class time coincided with his weekly visit
to the Federal Penitentiary, where he had made several
friends among the lifers, with whom he played poker (not
for stakes) and to whose reminiscences of life on the
outside he listened. His schedule was too busy to permit a
change, and he resolved to conquer the problem on his
own.

But the thing — whatever it was — that had got possession of his breathing redoubled its attack. A tight band, hard as iron, began to press about his throat and chest, and he was in actual pain, as well as discomfort. He began to dread his priestly functions as, when in fourth grade, he had dreaded school. Many days he had spent crouched in a cement culvert near the railroad tracks, and had had to forge letters purportedly from his mother, regretting that her son had been sick. That was a fact; he had had a belly-ache that had lasted a whole year. It had vanished on the day he was promoted to fifth grade and a new teacher. It was not so simple now. There was nothing to be promoted to.

He found it incredible that no one in the congregation seemed to hear his laboured breathing, or the thinness of the voice he managed to squeeze through the iron band that threatened to strangle him and nowadays jeered and jabbered at him, trying to jumble the prayers as he read them (he no longer trusted his memory). Sometimes he feared he had mouthed nonsense, or worse, and did not know whether to be relieved that it had been tactfully ignored, or to consider his parishioners demented, not noticing his gibberish. His anguish was extreme, and as afraid of it as he was of the enemy presence within him that caused it, he could speak of it to no one, not even to Ann.

Christmas was a nightmare, but he survived, getting through Midnight Mass like a person hypnotized. He had the impression during the Prayer of Humble Access that the thing had succeeded, it had choked him to death. Later, standing at the church door, wishing the joys of the season to friends and strangers, he saw that his existence depended not on his own perception of it, but on that of other people.

On Boxing Day, he did not take the girls skating, as he had done ever since they could remember. (They loved to skate with him. "Is that *your father?*" other children asked, gawking respectfully as Saintly skimmed by, at one with the ice and the bright transparent air.)

"I've forgotten how," Saintly said regretfully.

They stared at him in vexed disbelief. Emily, who was twelve years old and had a hot temper, said he was a mean old meanie-cat. Camilla, two years older, permitted her topaz eyes to brim, and said he had ruined their day. Ann came in and shooed them away to skate by themselves. Her eyes, so like Camilla's, were dark with worry.

"You're not yourself," she said.

She had no idea how frightening those words were.

"You must take a little holiday, the minute the annual meetings are all over," she told him. "We'll manage it somehow. Where would you like to go, and when?"

"Where" and "When" floated tantalizingly around the room. He could see them attaching themselves to various objects — tables, books, a scarlet poinsettia, the bright baubles on the Christmas tree.

The Sunday after Christmas, normally a lethargic one, brought out a large congregation to honour the bishop of the diocese, who was paying his yearly visitation to St. Jude's. He was a portly man, with a ready smile, and he had a habit of intoning his words so that his simplest remark seemed cloaked in authority. Richly mitred and robed, and clasping in his jewelled hand the gleaming pastoral staff, he had just begun his sermon — "At this season of the year, we think of God..." — when Saintly rose from his stall and disappeared into the sacristy. He hung up his vestments, put on his overcoat, fur hat and boots, and trudged across the snow-drifted lawn to the rectory, to slip numbly into bed. There he stayed, arms folded across his chest, scarcely speaking.

At his request, Ann kept away all visitors. Except for the bishop who, perhaps unable to conceive of himself as having other than a therapeutic effect upon a sick clergyman, marched up the narrow staircase, down the hall, and into the bedroom.

"I'm terribly sorry," Ann said, when the bishop had gone. "I couldn't stop him. He simply bolted past me."

"Who?"

"Oh, Saintly," she said reproachfully. "You couldn't not have noticed that the bishop was here. He's dull, but he's not invisible."

"Someone was here. I couldn't quite make out what he wanted. He seemed a harmless sort though."

The smile he gave her took the shape of the deep dark lines that in the past few weeks had been graven into his face. She suddenly saw that it was a clown's smile, and had to hurry out of the room, to cry in private.

It was given out that Saintly was suffering from overwork, and on the doctor's orders was taking a rest. Parishioners, distressed to hear that he had depleted himself on their behalf, flooded him with get-well cards and potted plants and bottles of Harvey's Shooting Sherry, light novels and puddings. They asked what they could do for the rector, would he like a portable television set? A new bathrobe? A vacation in Florida? A jigsaw puzzle?

"Does he care for lemon meringue pie?" asked the president of the Women's Guild, proffering one.

"I don't know if he cares for it. He eats it, if that's what you mean." This sharpness was uncharacteristic of Ann, but she was weary, and worried by her mysteriously ailing husband who in fact had that afternoon told her in a sober, judicious way that he cared for nothing and nobody. He had added that he was "very sorry".

Each morning she brought him his mail, and writing paper so that he could write thank you letters — he had always been punctilious about such things. But he wrote no letters, merely appended a line to a communication from the personnel manager of a trust company requesting a character reference for a prospective employee. "Judge not, that ye be not judged" Saintly scribbled in a hand that had all at once become large and ungainly. He put it in the stamped self-addressed envelope and gave it to Ann to mail.

After a month of leaden days and nights tortured by insomnia, Saintly called a psychiatrist whom he had met while taking part in a television panel discussion, "God or Psychiatry?" (Saintly had opted for God), and said in his courteous way that he would like to be admitted to a mental hospital.

Six weeks later he was ready to emerge, electro-shocked into new being. Dr. Brudenstein, a spry man with bright black eyes, had a consultation with Ann shortly before her husband was discharged. He had news, he said, that might be something of a shock to her. Certainly it would radically alter her way of life.

Ann sat bolt upright, bracing herself.

"Your husband," he continued, "has made a remarkable recovery. He is a walking advertisement for our treatment. But he can never, must never, does not want ever to go back to his old job. He no longer believes in God."

"Oh..." said Ann, on a long, relieved breath. It was Divine associations, then, that Saintly wanted to renounce, not domestic.

"Matter of fact," Dr. Brudenstein mused, tapping his cheek, "his trauma over Disbelief was the most convincing argument for Belief that I have ever encountered. All in all, a unique case."

The bishop, who had often spoken of Saintly as "a simple man of good faith", was perturbed to hear how matters stood. "He is having a dark night of the soul," he told Ann. Privately, he thought Saintly's behaviour excessive; if every clergyman took his belief—or disbelief—so seriously, the Church would be in a pretty pickle. He pressed a buzzer on his desk, and asked his secretary to bring him a cheque-book.

"What are we going to tell people?" asked Ann, watching his neat penmanship. "It's going to be a fearful shock to his parishioners. You've no idea how they depend on him. What if——" She stopped, picturing Belief disappearing from every suburban street, vanishing like water running down a hole.

"We intend to say that he is taking an extended leave of absence from his pastoral duties," the bishop smoothly replied.

"But it's a permanent leave," she cried, knowing Saintly wanted that understood. She took the cheque he handed her with a murmured thank you.

"Ah well, there is no need to labour the point, is there?" He patted her shoulder, and bade her remember that they always had a friend in him.

In the bus, going home, Ann looked at the cheque. One thousand dollars, from the bishop's discretionary fund. She realized what a comfort money was when you had nothing else, and tried to think of a way to make some.

When Saintly had been home for a few days, their great friend Simon Boyd came to see them. He too was a clergyman, several years younger than Saintly, and a man of considerable talent. Recently, a special post had been created for him. He was Consultant-at-Large to the Anglican communion, and flew about the globe, preaching, lecturing, consulting, setting up programs and projects, moderating panels, training people in Encounter-Group techniques, presiding over Group-Life-Labs.

"Delicious. What a treat," Ann said, tasting the Jack Daniels that Simon had brought back from San Francisco, where he had been the keynote speaker at a Church-World Institute.

Saintly drank apple cider with a cinnamon stick in it.

He was in tranquil spirits, though not talkative, and excused himself early. He would play Scrabble with the girls, he said, and if it did not seem rude, go to bed early. He explained that he was dreaming a continued story, each episode of which began promptly at nine o'clock.

Ann was glad of a chance to confide in Simon, who had always seemed part of the family. Simon had already considered most of the problems she faced, and had solutions for some of them. For instance, as they would soon be leaving the rectory, they must live in his house until they found something to their liking. He would be gone for three months on a tour of war-and-famine – struck Asian countries. (As far as he was concerned, he added, they could live in his house permanently.) And Saintly should apply immediately for early retirement on grounds of ill health.

"He wants to be deposed," Ann said.

"How like him. But we must dissuade him from doing anything rash."

"I'm afraid he'll insist. He'd think it dishonest to go on tacking Reverend in front of his name, getting sent free tickets to religious spectaculars, and turkeys at Christmas from the undertakers, that sort of thing. Being deposed would clear the air. Of course it'd be disillusioning to an awful lot of people."

"That's a delicate point. Best not to use it as an argument, I think. We'll take a practical line. If he insists on being deposed he'll lose his pension rights, and certain other fringe benefits — low-premium insurance, the girls' tuition at their school. They're minor, but they add up. Let me talk to him, it's easier for me."

"You won't worry him about the girls, or me, will you? I've been thinking, my godmother owns that new boutique, the Just Fancy. She might give me a job, she's crazy about Saintly. I'll buy a nifty outfit and get my hair cut at Sassoon's — I can use the bishop's money, it'll be an investment — and present myself to her."

"Fine. But you'll still need the pension. It may be a while before Saintly gets on his feet. What do you think he has in mind to do? Has he talked about it?"

"He's thinking of going into the odd-job business. He's going to hang out a sign saying 'No Job Too Small'. I thought No Job Too Big would be more of a lure, but he disagreed. Have you any ideas?"

"I'm toying with one. Let me see if it comes to anything. I'll be doing a bit of groundwork while I'm away."

Surprisingly, Saintly put up no resistance to remaining a clergyman in good standing, if not in good health. "Why not? It's just money."

Simon and Ann concealed their satisfaction.

"The Pension Fund," Saintly went on, "has probably done more to hold the church together than any amount of dogma. The Church's one foundation, you might call it. I understand they've pretty much scrapped the Virgin Birth, and other miracles, but they'll never scrap the Pension Fund. What other security is there?"

"You shouldn't bait Simon like that. You're taking advantage of him. You probably know that Dr. Brudenstein said we mustn't argue with you."

"Dr. Brudenstein lacks confidence in his cures." Saintly

smiled. Those deep dark lines would probably never disappear from his face, but now, refashioned by his smile, the effect of them was, unexpectedly, mirthful.

Ann sold all their non-essential possessions to a second-hand dealer. The rest they stored in Simon's basement. Even with the pension money, and Ann's part-time job and Saintly's odd jobs, the going was difficult. They agreed they could not stay for ever in Simon's house, and before he came back they had used the rest of the bishop's money to rent a little house, built apparently of various thicknesses of cardboard, in another part of the city. Harmonyville, it was called.

"Horrorsville," Camilla glumly renamed it.

"We can pull the shades down, and then we won't know where we are, will we?" Ann said, in what she hoped was a bright persuasive tone.

"Since when is getting lost a groovy idea?" asked Emily.

But they were resilient children, and at least they did not have to change schools as well as neighbourhoods. By bus and subway they travelled daily to the excellent school they had always attended (tuition free, as the daughters of a clergyman). Ann, thanks to the efficient urban transport system, was no farther from the Just Fancy than she had been before.

By picturing them all lying horribly maimed in hospital beds, she sometimes managed to convince herself that things could be worse.

Saintly regretted having to leave his most leisurely job, walking a widow's poodle for two half-hour periods a day. His responsibility on these excursions was to see that the poodle — a grey and grizzled old fellow — performed, as his mistress put it. She was hard of hearing and, when Saintly and the dog returned, would shriek from the kitchen window, "Well, did he perform? One and two?"

"All satisfactory," Saintly would usually call back. Sometimes he could report only one performance, and he and the dog would have to promenade again. The dog's lack of concern for a workingman's wages amused Saintly. "You're making me work overtime, *gratis*," he said. The old fellow stretched his lips in the way poodles do.

"How do you think Saintly will take to it?" asked Simon.

"Gosh, I don't know," Ann said, thoughtfully sipping her wine. The two of them were having lunch at a French restaurant to celebrate Simon's return. Saintly was unable to join them. He was at his Monday job, clipping greens at an expensive golf club, in return for which he got $2.50 an hour and the privilege of using the course when there were no members on it. "I don't see how he can write prayers when he doesn't believe in God."

"Matisse, busy at work on that chapel, made a point of saying he didn't believe in God."

"Religious subjects have always lent themselves to art."

"Writing prayers is an art, isn't it? Fortunately for their congregations most clergymen still fall back on the prayer book, but there's a multitude of twentieth-century conditions the prayer book doesn't address. Think of the Astronauts. Why, Saintly might write a prayer for the first man on the moon. Not that I expect him to plunge instantly into interstellar affairs, or even international. There's always a need for special-occasion prayers. I have no gift for them, and Saintly has always been very obliging.

I have a file of his compositions, and I've never used one that I haven't been asked for copies. Some I've used, with minor changes, for several events. One that he wrote for the Junior hockey finals I've used for a bonspiel in Manitoba, a soccer match in Ceylon and a baseball game in Tokyo. In each case, by the way, the right team won. Anyway, on this last trip, whenever I used one of his prayers, I told people about Saintly. Forced by ill health to retire, charming wife, two young daughters, having a bit of a struggle. I suggested that a little gratuity wouldn't be in bad taste along with a request for a prayer. Mind you, I don't think there'll ever be big money in it, but...."

"Every penny counts," Ann finished. "How I hope Saintly will agree to try it."

At first Saintly said no, flatly. "I'd rather sell patent medicines at a county fair. Besides, I've lost the formula."

"It's easy enough to find it," Simon said. "Brush up on your prayer book."

Saintly's face went still, as it had done in the bad days, the lines deepening in it, the grey eyes remote.

Seeing this, Simon said, "It was only a suggestion."

"It seemed a super idea, odd-jobwise," Ann said, "but if you feel you can't do it...." She sighed, and there was silence for a moment in the cardboard parlour.

Saintly got up and stretched, a long long stretch, as if he were loosening every muscle and joint in his body. "I'll give it a try," he said. "Tomorrow I'll start the prayer-wheel turning."

Simon and Ann looked at each other.

"I picked up a few orders in England, on my way

home," Simon said, matter-of-factly. "Unfortunately, with the exchange unfavourable, the total was only $7.86. Still, it's a start."

"The lord loveth a cheerful giver," Saintly said, handing the money to Ann.

By the following noon, Saintly had finished his first assignments. He had covered the opening of a strawberry festival ("...Thou, who hast given us of Thy bounty, look affably upon this seasonal gathering, and grant that these kindly fruits of the earth may bear fruit in kindliness in our parish..."), Closing Day in a boys' school ("...bestow upon us the courage to be generous in triumph, of good spirit in defeat, swift in the service of justice, uncompromising in the pursuit of excellence..."), the launching of a fund drive for a civic art gallery ("...may our eyes be opened to see in these works of art, fashioned by human hands, a reflection of the everlasting art of the universe, fashioned by Thy divine hands..."). Finally, he provided a blessing for a new recreation room in a home for the elderly ("...Thou, who hast created this world for Thy pleasure, graciously direct us in our recreation, that it may be honourable, amiable, and always pleasing in Thy sight...").

Finished, he stamped and addressed the envelopes, and sent them air mail to their destinations. "My prayers fly up, my thoughts remain below," Saintly said to himself, dropping the letters into the scarlet pillar-box on the corner. He hurried home, changed his clothes and went off to do his Wednesday yard job for a retired Naval captain and his wife, who gave him tea on the back stoop at four o'clock, out of a slightly chipped blue willow cup.

For some months Simon continued to bring the prayer orders back from his travels, scribbled on bits of paper and tucked in his pocket along with crumpled bills. One evening, he said, "I think we've got the thing off the ground now. I picked up fifteen orders in Chicago over the weekend, and several people — apparently in no immediate need of a prayer — expressed an interest. I left your name and address with the Episcopal Book Centre, and they'll deal directly with you. And if that goes smoothly, we can hook into the whole network of church bookstores and conference centres."

"It makes it seem less fly-by-night," Ann said, encouragingly.

"I rather liked that part of it. On the other hand, a nuisance for you, Simon, having to do the leg work."

"It was no trouble. It was just getting beyond me, as I hoped it would. You'll do better if people can reach you directly, particularly in emergencies. Do you remember doing a job for a civic art gallery in Leeds? Not only did their drive go over the top within weeks, but they were given a Henry Moore for the garden."

"Goodness," said Ann, "I never thought of your getting results, did you, Saintly?"

"If you don't mind" — Saintly turned to Simon — "I'd rather not hear about results."

"Well, Simon can tell me," Ann said. "I adore magic, things like prayers being answered, extra-sensory perception, all that kind of thing."

"I suppose you are both too young to remember the heyday of the magic lantern." Saintly leaned back in his chair, fingers laced across his chest. "When I was a child, I always attended the Wednesday evening Lenten lectures delivered by my father, and illustrated by slides that came, each week, in a black box secured with leather straps." He paused, then went on in the voice — at once ironic and rueful — that was peculiar to his reminiscing. "During pauses in the narration of the missionary journeys of St. Paul, I could hear the hum of the carbon arc lamp. One Wednesday evening, I glanced at my father's senior warden. In the pale light, he looked liverish. I said to myself, Mr. Frampton will die before this day is done. Late that night the telephone rang in the rectory. Mr. Frampton was dead. I felt guilty. I had been responsible for his death. I also killed Mr. Dawkins, the plumber. One Sunday, in a rage because my head refused to memorize the Collect for the day, I hurled my prayer book to the ground and, under my breath, muttered an oath. At that exact moment, Mr. Dawkins walked by. My murderous rage had its effect. Only hours later, the call came. Mr. Dawkins had passed on to the happy home of all plumbers and steam-fitters, where the living waters ever flow with never a hitch in the works."

He smiled, almost apologetically, while they laughed.

Naturally, there were problems to be ironed out with the bookstores. Managers wanted Saintly to quote prices. Did he charge by the word, they inquired, and were there discounts for job lots? Two religious book publishers, one Presbyterian, the other Roman Catholic, wrote that if he had a book in mind they would be happy to discuss it with him. Such requests Saintly ignored. He filled requests for prayers (without a set fee) and that was all. Then an unforeseen complication arose. Bookstores began allowing customers to put prayers on their charge accounts.

Simon, in Washington to chair a conference on Sex in the Christian Society, got word that there had been a sudden lag in prayer production. The orders, a puzzled saleswoman told him, were not being filled, not even being acknowledged. Customers were disappointed, especially several congressional representatives who had now and then to address a sectarian group, and found Saintly's felicitous phrases invaluable. It sounded ominous, and as soon as Simon got home, he hurried out to see Saintly.

"Look," he said, taking a business-like tack, "there seems to have been a bit of a snafu. Has anything gone wrong?"

"It's the charge-account system. Charge accounts are fine for department stores and oil companies, but they're no good for prayers."

"I see what you mean," Simon said, relieved to hear this simple explanation. "After all, you can't keep books with God."

"I don't know about that. But I know I can't write prayers without cash. I'm not sure what the connection is, but there it is."

"Wouldn't you even take on a charity case?" Ann looked at him, dismayed.

He shook his head. "Prayer is out, as a charity. And on a charge-account basis."

"It's so unlike him," Ann said later, with a troubled air. "Can you imagine Saintly demanding money, and for prayers, of all things? How can he do it? He's never cared about money."

"That's exactly it," Simon said. "Worthless prayers for worthless money. If he gave them away — don't you see? — he'd be implying that they were worth giving, that he had something to give. And who knows, perhaps prayers that people buy, cash on the line, have more efficacy than the ones they get for nothing, or on a pray-now, pay-later basis." He added, reassuringly, "Put it this way. There's no doubt that Saintly would help a blind man across the street. It's simply that he wouldn't pray for his safe passage."

Restored to a pay-to-pray basis, Saintly's facility returned. His mail daily increased in volume, and registered and special delivery letters came to be a nuisance, requiring that Saintly leave the "dinette" where, using a straight pen, and ink, he wrote the prayers on lined foolscap.

"Jeez," said the postman, a bent old man whose jacket reeked of cigarette smoke, "looks like you've got one of them mail-order rackets going."

"Some might say so," Saintly agreed, sprawling his name on the receipt book.

Every evening Saintly handed Ann the money that had come in that day.

"We'll have to keep track of it for the income tax, I suppose," she said. "It's amazing how these dribs and drabs mount up. Of course, the real turning point was that bishop. He uses up prayers like Kleenex."

This particular bishop, prelate of a rich metropolitan diocese in the United States, was noted for his mellifluous voice and stunning left profile. These gifts, which had originally helped raise him to his high office, now made his presence *de rigueur* at many smart secular functions. Wherever he went, nowadays, went one of Saintly's prayers. His secretary provided Saintly, at the beginning of each month, with a cheque and a copy of the bishop's official engagement calendar. Marvelling at the man's endurance, Saintly provided invocations or blessings for lunches and dinners honouring everyone from St. George the dragon-slayer to the widow of an art-collecting multi-millionaire. And many other events — a Charity Ball (" . . . we humbly ask that Thou, having granted us time to dance, and music, will grant us grace also, that our every step may please Thee . . ."), the launching of an America Cup contender (" . . . if it be Thy Will, command Thy fair winds to follow this vessel over the moving face of the deep, and bring her, in honour and safety, through every trial . . ."), the dedication of a new dormitory in a famous women's college (" . . . pour down the light of Thy wisdom upon these honourable women, that they may shine delectably among the polished corners of Thy temple . . .").

Of this last prayer, Simon, when guest-preaching at the college some months later, heard high praise, and was assured that never in the distinguished history of the college had there been such a wealth of brains and talent and beauty as there was in the new dormitory.

Ann was charmed to learn that.

"I constantly run into people," Simon went on, "who've subscribed to Saintly's prayers and had positive answers. Others are equally pleased with the wait-and-see response. I cite a fruit farmer on the Niagara peninsula who had ordered a prayer against an early frost. There was an early frost, and he lost his crop. He was desperate. Then along came a Buffalo millionaire who wanted to turn gentleman farmer, and was prepared to pay a whopping price. Result: the fruit farmer and his wife have bought a place in Florida, where they've always wanted to live and where frosts are few. He asked me to say that the welcome mat will be out for any of you, any time."

In 1972, the Gwynns moved into a different income-tax bracket, and into a different house. It was perched on the edge of a wooded ravine, and they got it for a song, because it was big and old and badly in need of repair, and in a neighbourhood no longer fashionable. Saintly's odd jobbing had made him handy with tools and paintbrush, and he repainted exterior and interior, rebuilt the railing around the wide verandah that enclosed three sides of the house, repaired shutters and cabinets, and on a whim, fixed the dumb-waiter that wheezed its way up from the old kitchen where there was a wood-burning stove, the very thing for his bread-baking.

There was a tower, too, which he used as a workroom. He had a table and chair, and a cot for catnapping, and a shelf on which he kept paper, ink and fresh pen nibs, a World Almanac, and a Liturgical calendar on which were marked all the High and Holy days, and the saints' days, both red letter and black.

There, every morning, he wrote prayers.

In the afternoon, he prepared the dinner — Ann's job

was full-time now, and Saintly did most of the household chores — and later worked in the garden. He espaliered peach trees against the old brick wall, and planted roses of every colour and size, early-blooming and late-blooming. Their fragrance filled the air all summer long, attracting brown velvet honey-bees and butterflies in elegant dresses. When he had finished his work, Saintly stretched out in a deck chair.

Of necessity he was becoming something of a recluse, but he did not seem to mind. As word of his miraculous gifts spread, requests for his time and services increased. He was adamant, however, against public appearances and interviews, and could not be coaxed by any of his former colleagues into addressing even the smallest gathering.

One day, though, he found wandering about in the house a female reporter from one of the city newspapers, and mistaking her for a harmless prowler, fell into conversation with her. That is, she conversed, and inspired by his attentive listening discovered in herself intuitions and perceptions she had not known she possessed. He made tea and cinnamon toast for her, and heard the story of her life. Upon leaving, she realized that she had not got the scoop she had come for. This man whose privacy (she now realized) she had grossly invaded, had scarcely said a word. But she had something else. She had on the neat little tape-recorder that she carried in her bag an unusually interesting monologue. She had not realized until then that her own life was worth writing about, but finding that it was, she made it into a novel which enjoyed a small critical success. She sent a copy to Saintly, affectionately and gratefully inscribed. Saintly, who did not recognize her name — she had given him a false one — said after reading it that it was odd, he had heard the identical story before.

The girls, in their final years of school, flourished, and took their father's peculiar notoriety in stride. Friends who visited them for weekends envied them their parents, seeing Ann as a liberated woman who laughed easily and warmly, and was also good looking. Of Saintly, a friend of Camilla's said, frankly, "I thought he'd be some kind of *creep*, instead I meet this really sweet cat that pays *attention* to me and says what do *I* think of things? Oh, wow, if my father caught me meditating in full lotus position he'd say why didn't I go play tennis or do something *normal*. Your father just went on making waffles. He's really tuned in."

During Spring vacation, the girls went to a "retreat" for high-school students, superintended by one of Simon's spin-off groups.

"How was it?" Saintly asked, when they returned.

"Super," Camilla said. "Really out of sight. We had this worship service at sunrise where everybody got up and danced, or spoke a haiku. You didn't have to, but if you wanted to it could be about anything. It didn't have to be about a drop of dew on a blade of grass. One guy did a neat one, about his Vespa. Then we had meditation, and discussion groups about drugs and sex and politics and does life have any meaning."

"And what did you conclude?"

"Yes and no," Emily said. "That chicken pie smells yummy. Say grace, Cam, it's your turn."

"God's dead/Pass the bread."

"Pass the bread, please," Ann said, in mild reproof. "I must say I don't think that qualifies as a grace. It rhymes, and that's about all."

"Also, it's *passé*," Emily put in. "What about, Buddha's neat/Let's eat."

"That one rhymes, too," Saintly said, approvingly.

The theological picture had changed considerably since Saintly had lost his Belief. The death-of-God movement had peaked, and its heyday was over. Death itself was beginning to attract wide attention. Many new varieties of religious experience were being undergone. A close personal friendship with Jesus was popular in some circles, particularly among young people. Groups of businessmen met for breakfast at Holiday Inns, and began their day with prayers and hymn-singing; they testified that their career opportunities were markedly improved. Out of the East came messiahs with rich smiles and large motor cars and new recipes for spiritual well-being, often involving eccentric diets. Anthropologists returned from primitive societies converted to primitive faiths that required the use of hallucinogens, and a sloughing off of those inhibitions imposed by "civilization". Baptism by immersion became popular in churches where formerly a drop of warm tap water had sufficed. Lakes, rivers and streams were awash with saved souls, and so were the harbours, dotted with graceful sailing vessels, of several fashionable resorts. Churches that were *au courant* set aside a room as a *zendo*. Faith-healing and glossolalia were commonplace. Love-Ins and Pray-Ins were staged in urban cathedrals. In sophisticated parishes radical chic prevailed; mass was celebrated in private houses at the cocktail hour, with champagne and imported biscuits spread with *pâté* substituting for the conventional wine and wafers. Everywhere, God was being forced out of the stultifying confines of church buildings and into the world where He could become an Activist.

The rector of Saintly's former parish was a live-wire type, who preached the Social Gospel. "It's scold, scold, Sunday after Sunday," complained the (former) president of the Women's Guild, the very one who years earlier had wondered if Saintly cared for lemon meringue pie, and who still came to call now and then, bringing something home-baked for the Gwynns. "One week he scolds us for sitting in a nice warm church when we ought to be down at the steel mill where they've been having the strike, and the next week it's because we're not out at the penitentiary protesting about that hijacker who had the unhappy childhood. I'd like to hijack him! *And*," she drew a breath, "the latest is we're supposed to go to dirty movies, did you ever hear the like? He says we're too smug. That Marlon Brando! I'd like to smug him!" Her eyes flashed with daring.

The market for prayers climbed steadily. It was on the rise everywhere, Simon reported. In the United States, an Episcopal clergyman, chaplain of a large university, published a book of original prayers. Entitled *Let's Hit It Together, Jesus*, the book was selling like pizza from coast to coast, and its author was a frequent guest on television talk shows. He was also photographed for the newspapers as he went about his affairs, leading a march against the war in Vietnam, hammering on the door of an off-off-Broadway theatre closed because its current production had been banned as obscene, in exhortation with a fix on upper Broadway. (The fix had *his* face turned away from the camera.) Asked by a magazine writer what he thought of the Reverend Gwynn, the Canadian prayer writer, the swinging clergyman said, "I don't doubt he's sincere, but he isn't into the Seventies. His prayers are irrelevant."

"This really makes me barf," Emily said, disgustedly, handing the magazine to her father.

"That's a very nice shrub he's wearing," Saintly said, studying the picture of the bearded man in the clerical collar.

"He'd better not try to put you down! Calling you 'sincere'! What a twerp."

In fact the published prayers only whetted the public appetite for personalized prayers. The telephone rang so often with long-distance and local calls that the Gwynns had to ask for an unlisted number. It made him feel unreal, Saintly said, to talk to clients, and besides, he was often confused with Dial-a-Prayer, a tape-recorded service sponsored by a life insurance company. "It can't be good for their business," he said to Ann. "What kind of advertising is that? You're promised a prayer, and instead you get a sleepy voice croaking out Hullo, and waiting to hear who's calling."

Thanks to intermittent strikes in the Postal Service, Saintly had periods in which to catch up with back orders. But the price he paid was high when a strike was ended and the postman — this one young and sturdy — unloaded his overflowing sack in the front hall. He — and a few chosen friends — had a special ring to alert Saintly, who otherwise did not open the door.

The letters all had to be sorted and separated, as the wheat from the chaff. Those reporting satisfactory results — the first line was enough to clue Saintly in — were torn up and burned in the kitchen stove, along with crank mail accusing him of gulling the public or using the mails to defraud. There was also commercial correspondence, much of which entertained him. What a diversified world his solitary occupation touched upon! Astrologists peddled their horoscope services. Artists wanting to illustrate his prayers enclosed samples of their work, usually representations of saints with moping faces, barefoot and with squared-off toes (St. Francis outran all other saints six to one). A man with a divining rod suggested a partnership. A radio evangelist in distant Tijuana offered Saintly his mailing list, for a fat fee. He sent along a glossy 8 " by 12 " photograph, which showed that he bore a striking resemblance to a man who had once cheated Saintly in a used car deal.

Camilla, married to a biophysicist and living in Chicago, and Emily, still in college, exchanged newspaper items referring to their father. Camilla found an interview with a Milwaukee man who had grown rich in the plastic bag industry and purchased a racing stable. His horse won the Kentucky Derby, and dazed with triumph the proud owner declared that the victory had been due to "a prayer

I bought from a minister up in Canada, some kind of saint." And Emily sent Camilla a small dispatch from Rome, containing the news that Libera Leone, touted as the successor to Sophia Loren, had found a new life through the prayers of "a defrocked priest in Ontario, Canada." "Pretty rococo!" Emily scribbled in the margin.

Such tidbits brought reporters, photographers and curiosity seekers scampering to the Gwynn's house, hoping for a word with Saintly, or a glimpse of him. It was remarkable that in all these years he had avoided being photographed or interviewed. A cabinet minister, whose wife was a client of Saintly's, called him "Canada's most closely guarded secret."

Simon said that Saintly had become a cult figure. "They've all but canonized him," he told Ann.

"Well, as long as they don't bring a halo," she said. "Not that he'd have anywhere to wear it. He doesn't dare step out of the house now, except to work in the garden. If people sneak in and find him he pretends he's the gardener. He puts on a Scots accent, you'd swear it was the real thing. But it *is* getting difficult. A few weeks ago some people came in their wheel-chairs. I felt like a dragon, saying they couldn't see him. I gave them pencils and paper and they wrote out their orders and trundled off. One of them came back not long ago with a hooked rug she had made for Saintly. It had a little church on it, of all things."

"Was she in her wheel-chair?"

"No, on foot," Ann said casually. "She was using a cane.

But you can see, it's getting out of hand. And Saintly's been looking tired, lately. It's depressing work. Sometimes when he gets behind I help — not with the prayers, just with sorting letters — this pile is people who want to be healthy, this pile is people who want to be rich, this one's people who want to interfere with their children's lives, that one's people who want a change in something, the climate, or the government. It all boils down to I Want. No one orders a prayer that says God, how marvellous! or You're simply divine! or This is absolute heaven! Which is what I hear all day long at the Just Fancy. I'm not being funny," she protested, when Simon laughed. "When you come right down to it, it must be very depressing, hearing all those I Want's, and Give Me's."

"For Saintly?"

"For God, too. Not that I'm comparing the two," she hastily added.

Simon looked troubled. "I had no idea how the thing would snowball," he said. "If I'd known, I'd have thought twice before suggesting it."

"It's not your fault the prayers keep getting answered," she said firmly. "The original suggestion was a perfectly good one."

One rainy October morning when Saintly sat down at his table in the tower to begin his day's work, fatigue overcame him. He cast a longing glance at the cot, but said to himself, sternly, "Look to the ant, thou sluggard," and began to write. The pen in his hand was a cruel weight, and his fingers cramped, holding it, pushing words across the page. In some perplexity he pushed his chair back and got up. Immediately, the fatigue lifted.

He spent the rest of the morning chopping kindling and piling it beside the wood on the back porch. Finishing, he considered raking the lawn — a high wind the night before had brought down a fresh fall of leaves. Instead, he strolled about, stepping delicately to avoid crushing the leaves, whose beauty all at once amazed him. He thought he had never before noticed their rhythmic shapings, the brilliance of their colours. In his mind's eye he saw the black metal box of Reeve's paints he had been given for his tenth birthday, each glistening cube with its name printed beneath it — Crimson Lake, Rose-Madder, Burnt Sienna, Ochre, Umber, Vermilion. And there they all were, those euphoniously named colours, burning softly in the grey air. What a fiery language they spoke! How splendid Nature was in her profligacy, all those leaves gorgeously rotting to replenish the earth! In a few months the unleaving trees would again be dense with foliage and sweet with bird song.

Standing there, he heard in his head the high-pitched voice of the horned prairie-lark, saw it rising from the stubbled prairies in swift undulating flight, disappearing into the vast sky, still singing.

Joy overwhelmed him. He thought of leaping into the air, climbing a tree, getting on his old bike and riding no hands down the hill. From the ravine gardens came the smell of wood smoke. His whole childhood with all its innocent pleasures and secret sorrows flashed upon him as he stood in his autumn garden, and he was caught not in memory but in a suspension of it. Time past and time present were fused; for that instant he seemed to stand outside himself, looking into the heart of things. He felt that he had been reborn.

But the next morning, and the morning after that, the same fatigue engulfed him, and his hand trembled under the weight of the pen. His fingers went numb, and sharp pains shot up into his arm. The words were there, but he could not inscribe them.

The family doctor said it was a simple case of writer's cramp. He prescribed muscle relaxants, and advised Saintly to use a tape-recorder for the time being, and then purchase an electric typewriter.

Ann brought Camilla's old tape-recorder downstairs. She switched it on, to see that it was in working order, and found that it was harbouring a vivacious reading by Camilla and Emily from *The Importance of Being Earnest*, the scene in which Gwendolyn and Cecily meet, vow eternal friendship and part on icy terms, all in the space of ten minutes. Saintly laughed so hard that he had to sit down.

"There we are," Ann said. "I'll get a supply of tapes and all you have to do is talk into this saucy little gadget. I'll get the stuff typed up and you'll be back in business."

After a moment, Saintly said, regretfully, "I'm afraid I can't do it. I don't know why, but I know I can't do it."

The mail piled up. Ann asked Saintly did he have any old prayers around that she could copy? "At least people would be getting something for their money."

Saintly, who was punching down a batch of bread dough, said, "Wouldn't it be simpler to send the money back?"

The prayer wheel, after ten years, had stopped turning.

Camilla and her husband, and Emily and her boyfriend, a sculptor who worked in welded steel, came to spend the New Year's holiday with their parents.

"What's happened to Father?" asked Emily, when Saintly had gone down to the kitchen to check on the goose he was roasting. "He looks so young!"

Ann took a good look at him when he came back. How had she failed to notice? Those deep dark lines had almost disappeared from his face. Perhaps, after all, they had only been sketched in. For a moment she regretted that. She had grown fond of the clown's smile.

After dinner the young people went down to the ravine rink to skate. It was a cold, still night. The sky gave the impression of having lowered itself and was full of stars that quaked and trembled just beyond arm's reach.

Camilla, waltzing with Emily's boyfriend, was the first to see Saintly. "Look!" she cried.

"Is that your *father*?" he asked, respectfully, stopping to watch as Saintly stroked in long *legato* across the ice, as easy as a bird in flight.

He came to a stop beside the four of them, his skates sending up little jets of ice dust.

Emily said, "You told us you'd forgotten how!"

Skating backwards, he described a circle around them, in herringbone pattern. "If you live long enough," he said, "everything comes back to you." Tipping his head, he looked up at the starry sky. His breath smoked in the frosty air.

Naturally, there was a considerable flurry when word got about that Saintly, having ceased to write the wonder-working prayers, had come out of retirement. Several parishes expressed an interest in calling him as rector; Saintly referred them to the bishop, who was pondering his application for reinstatement as an active priest. He had appointed a committee to consider Saintly's "case" and together they screened the letters that poured into the episcopal offices.

Former parishioners wrote of Saintly as a kind man and dedicated pastor, and employers of his odd-job days remembered him as honest, reliable, hard-working, and a gentleman. The widow whose dog he had walked said that if her old poodle could come back from the grave he'd have nothing but good to say of the Reverend Mr. Gwynn. Countless clients, rising above personal disappointment at the turn events had taken, vouched for his integrity. A woman in Yonkers, N.Y. testified as follows:

> At first when I didn't win the State Lottery I was real disappointed, but I'd kind of got used to saying the prayer the Reverend wrote for me so I just kept on saying it. The words are so nice. And I guess I've found that Spiritual Fortune he wrote about, and it's better than anything money can buy. Believe you me. It's like they say, I've got a "new lease" on life, and I'm going to say that prayer for the rest of my days.

There was a good deal of unfavourable criticism, too. Cynics — among them several of his fellow clergymen — said that the prayer business had been falling off and he wanted In again. Skeptics debated whether he had falsely claimed magical powers or magical powers had been

falsely attributed to him. A psychology journal interviewed a hundred and twenty-seven persons who claimed
that their prayers had been answered, in an effort to prove
that the whole thing had been an example of human chain-
reaction; people believed something because other people
believed it. They cited flying saucers, the Abominable
Snowman and the Loch Ness monster as other examples
of the same phenomenon. The piece, entitled *Build a Better
Mouse Trap . . .*, took up most of the issue, and contained
such (unverifiable) statements as, "For a buck I bought a
prayer that put my kid through dental school."

"I wish I knew where he practised," Saintly said. "I'd
beat a path to his door. I have a tooth that wants filling."

"*You* may think it's funny," Ann said, as she gave the
magazine to Simon, who hadn't seen it, "but I'm fed up
with all these explanations and speculations. At least good
old Dr. Brudenstein didn't blab. He just said yours was a
unique case. Goodness, it seems no time since he said that
to me." She dropped a kiss on Saintly's hair, which was as
thick as ever but now snow-white.

"You're a hot sermon topic, too," Simon said, glancing
up from his reading. "Did you notice last Saturday's paper?
'Prayer: Positive Reinforcement?' 'Magic or Mass?' 'Is
Your Prayer Necessary?' 'Doubting Thomas; True
Believer?'"

"Those people need an answering service," Saintly said,
spreading honey on a toasted scone.

"Do be serious," Ann said, laughing. "Couldn't you
make up one simple clear statement that would satisfy
everybody?"

"One simple clear statement that would satisfy everybody," Saintly repeated, tipping back in his chair and frowning thoughtfully.

"Well — almost everybody."

"What about simply saying you've recovered your health?" Simon suggested. "No one can quarrel with that."

"A capital idea!" Saintly got up, looking pleased. "In fact I wonder I didn't think of it myself."

Simon was right. A man's good health may be enviable, but unlike matters of conscience and belief, it cannot be disputed.

An enthusiastic young internist took down Saintly's case history, and put him through a battery of tests. A week later, when all the results were in, he pronounced Saintly fit as a fiddle.

The bishop, reassured, summoned Saintly to his office. He offered him a glass of sherry, and a cure of souls in a rapidly growing suburb. Saintly said he would like to have a week to think about it and talk it over with Ann. The bishop said he could take two weeks, or even three. Time, he declared, was relative. He advised Saintly to think of the past ten years not as time wasted or lost, but as a period of growth. Saintly, recalling that the clerical shirts and collars he had impulsively purchased that afternoon were a half-size larger than those he had discarded a decade earlier, said he thought there had been some growth.

The bishop then mused aloud upon enriching experiences and the unfathomable nature of the Divine Will. "As the poet Cowper puts it," he concluded, " 'God moves in a mysterious way, His wonders to perform.' "

Saintly finished the verse for him, pleased as always by the sturdy athletic feat implicit in the imagery. "'He plants His footsteps in the sea, And rides upon the storm.'"

He had not taken the poet's words as having a personal reference. It had never occurred to him to think of himself as a wonder.

At Sunnyside Villa

MRS. CAMERON'S ROOM AT SUNNYSIDE VILLA WAS A pleasant one, facing south, and with wide windows giving on lawn, border garden, and a planting of young maples. It was a semi-private room, furnished in matching pairs of beds, bedspreads, night-tables, lamps and dressers. From the walls on her side of the room Mrs. Cameron's son Malcolm had removed the reproductions of impressionist paintings and had hung in their place two small seascapes in water-colour, an engraving of Edinburgh castle, and a Japanese print of a woman in a scarlet kimono, curving bonelessly towards the looking-glass into which she gazed.

Into the frames of the pictures were tucked snapshots of infants, and children, and young people dancing at wedding parties, and there were others pinned to the bulletin board, along with greeting cards and messages written in Malcolm's sprawling hand, "Virginia will pick you up at five", "Leonie and Geoff at seven", "Betsy and Nell to tea at four", "Maria arrives Thursday", and so forth. The bulletin board rested against the pale blue wall behind the television set, the screen of which was covered by a child's painting showing an amiable-looking tiger strolling through a jungle. From the ceiling was suspended a mobile of baseball players, also the work of a childish hand. On the dresser there were boxes of chocolates, a bright tin box containing shortbread or fruitcake, and a decanter of sherry and four crystal glasses standing on a round silver tray. There were always fresh flowers or a flowering plant. Beside the cushioned armchair was a low bookcase, holding copies of *Scottish Field*, several art books, and a photograph album bound in green leather.

Every day Mrs. Cameron looked through the album, opening it first to the centre to study a photograph of a grey-haired man with twinkling eyes and mouth curved in a quizzical smile, and on the facing page, an enlarged snapshot of two black-haired laughing young men standing in dappled sunlight, each wearing the uniform of an officer in the Royal Canadian Air Force. Unlike the other people pictured in the thick album, whose changing appearance reflected the passage of time, these three seemed fixed for ever at a particular moment, as though, of them, mortal time had no further record.

Mrs. Cameron's room-mate was Mrs. Preston. On her side of the room hung prints of an Utrillo snow-scene, a Degas dancer, and a Monet garden. On her dresser were framed photographs of three children, glass jars of candy and a box of Peak Frean Digestives. There was also a philodendron and an arrangement of artificial flowers so lifelike that everyone bent to smell it. She had a television set that was turned on once a month when her grandchildren came to visit, and on Sunday afternoons when her son or son-in-law watched whatever game was in season.

Mrs. Preston was a small woman, talkative and easily

entertained, and with a good-humoured complacent little chuckle. In the mornings she sat in her wheel-chair, talking to Mrs. Cameron and watching passersby in the corridor. After lunch she went back to bed for the rest of the day and, lying there, enjoyed Mrs. Cameron's visitors, and talked on the telephone. Visiting by telephone, she called it, and sometimes when Mrs. Cameron's visitors had left she remarked that it was much easier for her friends to visit by telephone than to have to drag themselves all the way across Toronto in the bad weather. In the beginning, she had told Mrs. Cameron to feel free to use her telephone whenever she liked, but as Mrs. Cameron was unable to talk she could not accept the offer.

Mrs. Preston said that they made ideal room-mates, for she could talk but could not get about — she was badly crippled by arthritis and the longest journey she made was by wheel-chair to the beauty parlour in the main lounge — whereas Mrs. Cameron could get about though she could not speak. These days, however, Mrs. Cameron got about very little. She had made a resolute recovery from the stroke that twelve months earlier had locked her into a prison of silence and left her right arm useless — limp and discoloured it rested in a small leather sling — and she was soon walking again, with a cane, and putting whole sentences together. But a second stroke had undone her hard-won learning, reducing her vocabulary to two or three words, and seriously impaired her balance. She had fallen two or three times recently, and although she had not been injured, she was a source of worry to the nursing staff. She was no longer supposed even to get up from her chair unattended.

Twice in one day she got up without ringing for help.

Mrs. Preston had to ring *her* bell, and the second time the nurse was angry. "You are a naughty, stubborn girl," she said to Mrs. Cameron, who was rearranging a bouquet of flowers. Mrs. Cameron looked at first perplexed and then offended by the pert reprimand. That evening, when her niece Leonie and Leonie's husband, Geoff, left, the nurse put the guard rails up around Mrs. Cameron's bed. The next morning they strapped her into a geriatric chair.

Mrs. Cameron did not eat any breakfast, and did not smile at the nurses and aides on their morning rounds. She sat unmoving, steeling herself to endure the indignity.

"I believe you're angry," Mrs. Preston said. "That's something I never thought I'd see!"

Mrs. Cameron turned her head slowly, then raised her good hand in a fist and shook it in the air. Her silence was majestic, as if in her wrath she spurned words. She refused to eat her lunch, too, and the pretty young Jamaican girl who came to get her tray was rude to her. "You'll get sick," she said, "and then you'll be more trouble than ever."

"Don't you speak to her like that!" Mrs. Preston's thin voice quavered with indignation. "It's not the first time, either. I've a good mind to report you. Poor Mrs. Cameron is helpless to do so for herself. But my goodness, just because she can't speak you needn't think she's stupid. It's my opinion she was once a very intelligent woman."

Mrs. Cameron shifted slightly in her prison chair, looking straight ahead.

Malcolm came in at five that afternoon. Mrs. Cameron's eyes lighted, seeing him, and she tried to rise from her chair as she always did when she had a visitor. Then she burst into tears.

"Mother!" He knelt beside her, putting his arms around her. "What's happened?"

"It's that chair," Mrs. Preston said. "She's very upset about it. And last night they put the guard rails up on her bed."

He hadn't noticed the chair until then, and he sprang to his feet, a tall man, strongly attractive, with curly black hair rather long and slightly greying. He reached across Mrs. Cameron and rang the bell twice, sharply.

The head nurse, a kindly woman named Mrs. McDermott, explained to Malcolm, but he curtly brushed her words aside.

"Very well," Mrs. McDermott eventually said, "but just remember, Mr. Cameron, it's your responsibility if your mother forgets to ring her bell and falls and breaks a bone."

"Better a broken bone than a broken spirit!" he said.

Mrs. Cameron lifted her head high for the first time that day, and her green eyes shone with pride.

Malcolm took her fur-lined coat from the closet. "Let's hustle along," he said. "Virginia and the girls have gone to meet Maria's plane. Did you remember that she's coming today?"

"Oh...no," Mrs. Cameron said joyfully, then laughed, because she had meant to say yes. She pointed to the bulletin board on which Malcolm had written, "Thursday p.m., party for Maria, Friday p.m., 85th birthday party for you."

"What a treat it will be to see Maria again," Mrs. Preston said. "I do enjoy her visits. So does your mother."

Mrs. Cameron's bad arm had got stuck in the lining of her sleeve, and they had to start over again. She wobbled, leaning on her cane, and laughed at her predicament. Her laugh was still clear and sweet, like that of a light-hearted young woman.

Maria brought Mrs. Cameron back that evening. Mrs. Cameron rested in her chair, watching Maria with eyes that were delighted and utterly absorbed, as if she felt herself to be her daughter crossing the room with a light step to kiss Mrs. Preston, long plaid-wool skirt swirling, frail golden hoops dangling from her ears, voice soft, and effortless.

"You're such a breath of fresh air," Mrs. Preston said, clinging to Maria's hand.

"That's the good Canadian air," Maria said. "I bring only a cloud of Los Angeles smog."

Maria and the nurse got Mrs. Cameron ready for the night, taking her to the bathroom, choosing a nightgown, plumping up her pillows, smoothing cream on her face.

"Don't forget her Pampers," Mrs. Preston said. "She needs two at night, otherwise she's likely to soak the bed."

Maria seemed not to have heard her. "Such a pretty nightgown, Mother," she said "Is it the one Leonie gave you for Christmas?"

A faint light from the corridor fell across the foot of each bed. Mrs. Preston was reviewing the incidents of the day, as she liked to do before going to sleep. "That was very fine, what Malcolm said," she finished. " 'Better a broken bone than a broken spirit.' "

In the shadows, Mrs. Cameron raised her hand, signifying limitless appreciation of her son.

THE MAN WHO SOLD PRAYERS

"Of course," Mrs. Preston added, with her little chuckle, "they're not his bones, are they?"

To that, Mrs. Cameron made no reply.

That very night, Mrs. Cameron fell.

Mrs. Preston was wakened by the thump at the foot of her bed. She put on her light, and rang for a nurse. Mrs. Cameron was taken away in an ambulance.

Malcolm was with Mrs. Cameron when they brought her back a few hours later. She was asleep, and didn't notice when he put the rails up, click-click. He kissed her cheek and left her sleeping.

"Fancy her not breaking a bone! But that must be a dreaful cut over her eye," Mrs. Preston said, when the nurse was getting her up. "How many stitches did they take?"

"Just five. Poor lady, she's going to look like she walked into a door, though. It's a shame, that happening to her. She's one of our very nicest guests." On her way out, the nurse stopped at Mrs. Cameron's bed, adjusted the ice-pack on her brow, and tucked the rosy blanket in around her. Mrs. Cameron did not stir. Her face was ivory-pale except for the purple bruise around one eye. They had not put her wig on, and wisps of silky hair straggled across her fragile-looking skull.

She wakened when Maria came in, carrying a florist's box.

"Happy Birthday!" Maria embraced her. "I'm so sorry about last night, what rotten luck for you!"

"It wasn't luck," Mrs. Preston put in. "I don't mean to

interfere, Maria, but I think she should have those rails up, never mind what Malcolm says."

"It's already been decided," Maria said crisply. "My mother and Malcolm have discussed it."

"It was very upsetting to me. Such a shock!"

"'I'm sorry, Mrs. Preston." Not looking at her, Maria unfurled the green paper from the flowers.

"Oh, aren't they lovely!" Mrs. Preston looked at the long-stemmed irises, purple as night, and the tulips, yellow as the summer sun.

"You must both enjoy them." Maria sounded friendly again. She lowered the rail, and sat on the edge of the bed, holding her mother's hand. "The doctor says you can get up tomorrow, aren't you pleased?"

Mrs. Cameron widened her eyes, to show that she was, then winced, and her eyes dulled with pain. Maria stroked the white hairs across her head. "I'll give you a finger-wave. Remember when finger-waves were the rage?" Mrs. Cameron smiled, remembering. Then, distastefully, she touched the neck of the coarse hospital gown they had put on her. Maria took from a drawer a crimson shawl, embroidered in black and gold. With an effort, Mrs. Cameron raised her head, and Maria drew the shawl around her shoulders, and arranged it over her breast. "There! You look like a Greek queen."

Mrs. Cameron made a wry grimace, and her eyes blurred again, and closed. Maria sat in a chair pulled close to the bed, and opened the book she had brought. Mrs. Preston looked out of the window. Pale morning sunlight glimmered through the lightly falling snow.

After a while Mrs. Preston said, "I wish they'd clean up that mess on the floor. It's very upsetting to look at it."

Maria got up, looking shocked. "What mess?"

"Down there, at the foot of my bed. It's your mother's blood."

A small stain, about the size of silver dollar, darkened the blue of the carpet.

"I'm sorry," Maria said stiffly. "I'll tell them about it." She sat down again, with her book, and when her mother wakened she talked to her in a low voice, inaudible on the other side of the room.

"You should speak a little louder, so she'll understand," Mrs. Preston said. "They gave her something to make her sleep, and she's probably confused."

Mrs. Cameron frowned, and said, "*No.*"

"Did they give you a Mickey Finn, Mother? Or one of Malcolm's famous martinis?"

Mrs. Cameron smiled. She looked into Maria's eyes, and set about trying to speak to her. Listening, Maria studied her mother's face, her own drawn in concentration.

At last she said, "Bernard! You're asking about Bernard!"

Mrs. Cameron let out her breath, in relief.

"He's very well, he sent you much love. Did you get a postcard from him, last week? You're the only person in the world that he writes to, he's hopeless about writing...."

Mrs. Cameron gestured at the books on the shelf.

"Oh yes, Mother darling," Maria said, amused, "he writes books, but not letters."

"My son-in-law should be a writer," Mrs. Preston said. "He has such an imagination! But he doesn't have time to write. He has to work."

Maria and her mother smiled at each other.

"You're good at mind-reading," Mrs. Preston said to Maria. "But it takes the patience of Job, doesn't it."

"My mother is the one with patience."

"Malcolm has it, too."

"Oh, Malcolm has always had the disposition of an angel." Her voice was warm, as if it pleased her to praise her brother, but it changed as she added, "But not I. What a beast I was, always criticizing and complaining. And sulking! I was loathsome, wasn't I. You don't know how often I think about it, and wish...."

But Mrs. Cameron was shaking her head in protest. "No...no," she said, and reached for Maria's hand.

"I believe you really have forgotten," Maria said softly. "How *kind* you are."

The two old ladies slept most of the afternoon, and outside the snow fell and fell. Shapes of things, sounds — the little contented puff on which Mrs. Preston exhaled each breath, the tick of Mrs. Cameron's travelling clock on the night-table, footsteps and voices in the corridor — seemed unreal; all that was real was that silent-falling snow. Maria scarcely moved. Her face was wan and pensive, and with heavy eyes she looked up from her book at the snow falling out of the low leaden sky or at the flowers burning purple and gold in the hot still air.

Most often, she looked at her mother, studying her countenance as if it were new to her. Mrs. Cameron slept soundlessly, as always, her composure suggesting pride of spirit, modesty of person. Her sparse hair clung damply to her skull, the bruise had spread purple and brownish-yellow across one high cheek-bone, her lips, lightly closed, were parched. Even so, there was nothing pitiable about that face — unless life itself be pitiable from birth to death — for even in sleep it conveyed a sense of the richness its wearer had found in life, of gladness as well as grief.

Mrs. Cameron wakened slowly, dazedly putting a hand to her brow. When she was fully awake, Maria said, "Shall we get you prettied up? Malcolm and the girls will be here soon. Would you like to put your wig on? The old one, or the new one?"

Mrs. Cameron chose the old one, which was shabby but soft, and more becoming to her bruised and tired face than the smartly coiffed new one she had been given at Christmas.

Watching, Mrs. Preston said, "I must make an appointment to have my hair done. Such problem hair, it's so thick. I almost envy your mother, having none. Or almost none," she added, in polite afterthought.

Maria said quickly, "Would you like to look at a book, Mother?"

"My goodness, such a party!" said Mrs. Preston, accepting the glass of champagne Malcolm had poured for her.

Propped against her pillows, Mrs. Cameron looked at Malcolm, who was perched on the edge of her bed. Her eyes spoke as her tongue could not, of love, and she carefully raised her glass in a toast to him, and pretended to sip her wine.

"We've got a surprise for you," Malcolm said, putting his glass down and hugging his hands around one knee. "We've managed at last to find a new house. Actually, it's an old house...."

"Daddy, you're not telling it properly, let me tell,"

burst out Betsy, dancing with excitement, making the room vibrate. "It's got an apartment in it for you, Granny! You're going to live with us! It's so cool, you'll love it. Your door opens into a garden, and I'm going to plant it for you, full of roses, I think."

"Oh . . . *my*!" Mrs. Cameron brought the words out in joyous disbelief, looking from one to the other of them with luminous eyes. Malcolm cleared his throat, and tears shone in Maria's eyes, which were green, like her mother's.

"You won't mind if I plant a little *grass* in your garden, will you, Gran?" asked Flora, sixteen years old and named for her grandmother. She had a crackly voice, red cheeks, and long shining black hair.

"She's joking, Granny," Betsy said. "Daddy'd never let her."

Maria laughed, stroking Betsy's fair hair. "To your grandmother, grass still means lawn."

Flora started across the room to offer biscuits to Mrs. Preston.

"Mind you don't step in the blood," Mrs. Preston said.

"Ugh . . . what blood?" Flora grimaced, stopping short.

"Your grandmother's blood. Where she fell last night, by the foot of my bed."

Flora looked down at the small stain at which the maid, at Maria's request, had ineffectually scrubbed, and said disdainfully, "Rats! I thought maybe you'd had a murder in here."

"You'd have thought so, if you'd heard the thump." Mrs. Preston chuckled.

"Oh, my poor Gran!" Flora flew across the room and kissed Mrs. Cameron.

"You must be exhausted," Mrs. Preston said, when the nurse had settled Mrs. Cameron for the night. "So many visitors, so much excitement. And mercy, what a thing to spring on you, that you'll have to move! I suppose they've arranged everything, someone to take care of you, and so forth. They didn't mention that, did they. Maria looked very tired today, I thought."

Mrs. Cameron looked anxiously at her room-mate. "I...oh...no...."

Mrs. Preston went on talking, looking up at the ceiling and not at Mrs. Cameron, whose face was in a confusion of anxiety and agitation.

"...quite happy here at Sunnyside, quite content. That's what I tell my children, when they mention buying a bigger house. Kind as it is, I say, you mustn't sacrifice your lives, or your children's, to mine." She folded her twisted hands over her bosom, and added, musingly, "It's a pity, isn't it, that Malcolm didn't find that house earlier."

Mrs. Cameron had raised herself on one arm, and was desperately trying to speak, all the while directing a dark and piercing gaze at Mrs. Preston, a quite ferocious glare made more terrible by the bruise staining one side of her face, and the patch of tape on her brow, across which the few white hairs straggled. With a groan, she let her head fall back on the pillow.

Mrs. Preston, turning to switch off her bed-lamp said, "Never mind. Better late than never, Mrs. Cameron! I'm sure you'll like your new home very much."

When Maria arrived next morning, Mrs. Cameron was sitting in her chair. She was wearing her wig, and a woollen dress printed in shades of green, and a lacy white sweater. The bruise on her face was fringed in yellow. She had in her lap two letters that had just arrived, and her photograph album. She had not looked at her room-mate all morning.

"Good morning, Maria," Mrs. Preston said. "Isn't your mother a wonder? Up and dressed and fresh as a daisy. I was just saying to my daughter, on the telephone, that Mrs. Cameron's not one to be kept down."

Mrs. Cameron gripped Maria's hand, and her face worked as she struggled to speak. After a few minutes she gave up in frustration, and turned her head aside, trying to hide her tears.

Maria's frustration was evident, too. "If only you could tell me, if only I could understand! But never mind, it doesn't matter, does it, whatever it is, as long as . . . ." But Mrs. Cameron's eyes were looking deeply in hers, and Maria said in a different tone, "Except that it does matter, doesn't it, it matters terribly. You have something to say, and I'm too stupid to understand what it is. We keep saying we know how you feel, but we don't know at all, do we, only you know, and you can't tell us . . . ."

Mrs. Preston, watching them, had begun to cry too, and Maria went over and kissed her, and said, as if lightly, "What a bad effect I have on both of you! Here, we'll all have a chocolate, that'll cheer us up."

Mrs. Preston chose, with care, a coffee-cream. Mrs. Cameron had put her hand to her face, as if to shut out the sight of her daughter comforting Mrs. Preston. Her hand was still fine in shape, and the fingernails, pink and healthy, looked as if they had just been manicured.

Sitting down again, Maria looked through the photograph album with her mother. "Who is this?" she asked, of each picture, and when her mother approximated a name, congratulated her enthusiastically.

"You can certainly get a lot out of your mother," Mrs. Preston said. "I wish she'd talk to me like that."

Mrs. Cameron made an abrupt gesture, spilling loose pictures on the floor. She looked at Maria intently, as if by sheer will-power she could force her daughter to understand the words that tumbled about in her brain.

"What is it, Mother? Something's bothering you. What happened? Was someone unkind to you?" She appealed to Mrs. Preston. "Was anyone unkind to my mother? Do you know what's bothering her?"

Mrs. Preston shook her head. "She's been like that all morning. She's very upset about something."

Maria turned back to her mother.

Mrs. Cameron's eyes were dark and fierce, and her face trembled, and as Maria watched she picked up her cane and brandished it, actually brandished it, in Mrs. Preston's direction.

Maria looked aghast. "Oh, she doesn't mean you, Mrs. Preston! Of course you don't mean Mrs. Preston, do you, Mother."

Mrs. Cameron let her head sink back against the cushions. Her eyes were suddenly empty, and she lifted her hand in a vague way and touched her head.

"You want the other wig! That's what it is. I should have guessed."

But when Maria brought the other wig, Mrs. Cameron shook her head and gently motioned it away. Something had clicked shut behind her eyes.

"So it wasn't that," Maria sighed. "Never mind, you'll tell me about it later. Don't think about it now. Look at the icicles! Do you remember the icicles in Saskatchewan? Ten feet long and a yard wide...."

Obediently, Mrs. Cameron looked at the icicles outside the window, on which sunshine flashed, and she nodded thoughtfully, and politely, to show that yes, she remembered the icicles, the Saskatchewan winters of which Maria spoke. But the remoteness was still in her eyes. She seemed to have retreated to a place where in solitude she would recover herself, gather herself up to come back to the world in which people could talk, but could not understand.

Breaking off her bright conversation, Maria looked down at her mother and said, "You'll learn to talk again, we know you will. You did it before, you'll do it again."

Mrs. Cameron nodded. Her face was weary.

"Well, even if she can't talk she's a lovely person and I certainly enjoy her company," Mrs. Preston said. "I often tell people how lucky I am to have her for a room-mate."

Maria glanced at her mother and said in a polite, but rather uncomfortable voice, "I'm sure my mother feels the same way about you."

Mrs. Cameron gave Maria a look in which there was resignation, and approval. She seemed to be saying that in Maria's place she would have made the same response.

Maria and Malcolm brought Mrs. Cameron back earlier than usual that evening, and stayed for some time after she was in bed, talking to her. "I'll be back in exactly six weeks," Maria said, finally. "It seems a long time, but if I come then I can help with the moving. Besides, I want to be here when you step across the threshold."

Mrs. Cameron smiled, and raised her hand, to blow a farewell kiss.

The changes in Mrs. Cameron during the next two weeks had a kind of slow drama about them, and were reflected in the momentary shock in the eyes of the friends who came to see her. Her face was becoming pointed and narrow like that of a fox, and was, strangely, beautiful, with the ivory skin drawn tight across the bones from which flesh had dissolved. She sat as erect as ever in her chair, but sometimes there was a rigidity in her pose, as if she were impaled there. Sudden noises made her start and tremble. Occasionally she dozed off even when she had visitors, or a perplexed look came into her eyes, as if the faces people wore and the things they said were not related to what she was thinking about, were indeed intrusions upon her profoundly private consciousness, intrusions which her innate courtesy forebade her to rebuke.

In the third week she had a bad cough. She could not go out to Malcolm's house, but had to stay in bed and take antibiotics. She looked at the meal-trays with disgust, and Virginia and her niece Leonie took turns bringing lunch in to her. One day Virginia brought fresh strawberries in a white bowl, and heavy cream in a little silver pitcher.

"They're delicious," Mrs. Preston said, enjoying her share.

"Do eat some," Virginia begged. "They're special, they come from California."

Mrs. Cameron looked at her questioningly, and Virginia said, with a smile, "Yes, like Maria."

Mrs. Cameron put out her hand and touched the bowl tenderly, as if it were a beloved face.

Virginia looked at her thoughtfully, then turned to the bulletin board and read aloud what Malcolm had written,

" 'April 28th, Maria arrives, Moving Day, May 1st.' And it's already April 8th! You can start counting the days."

Mrs. Cameron nodded, and reached for her spoon. She ate two berries, slowly, then sank back, exhausted. The cut over her eye had healed to a thin line, and the bruise had disappeared. Her eyes these days had a sheen across them, and behind the sheen a depth that had not existed before. It was as if all she knew and understood existed in that depth, and gradually and without regret she was moving into it.

That evening when Malcolm came in, he said, "I've got a surprise for you, Mother. Maria's coming tomorrow."

"Oh...no," Mrs. Cameron whispered.

Malcolm bent abruptly, and kissed her.

In the morning Mrs. Preston reminded Mrs. Cameron and told the nurses that Maria was coming, and Mrs. Cameron chose to wear the green dress that was Maria's favourite. Whenever a nurse or an aide said, "I hear your daughter's coming today," Mrs. Cameron said, "Oh... no," and then smiled, because she had meant to say yes.

All the same, when Maria walked in, Mrs. Cameron gave a bewildered cry, as though Maria were the last person she had expected to see.

"Now I'll give you all the family news," Maria said, sitting on the footstool beside her mother's chair. But she seemed nervous, over-bright, and kept getting up, re-arranging the flowers she had brought, straightening things on the dresser, eating shortbread. "That's what I really came for," she said, "to gobble up Leonie's short-bread."

Mrs. Preston chuckled, and Mrs. Cameron smiled, but

Maria frowned, and said, "What a stupid joke, it's you I came to see."

When her lunch tray came, Mrs. Cameron turned her head away, as if nauseated.

"Do eat just a little," Maria said. "Won't you try the soup?" She held the spoon to her mother's lips, but at the touch of the metal Mrs. Cameron shuddered, and some of the soup dribbled down her chin. Maria wiped it off, and said, "Never mind. Save your appetite for dinner. Virginia's cooking a splendid salmon, just for you."

Mrs. Cameron slept after lunch, and Maria took a walk. The instant Maria came back into the room Mrs. Cameron's eyes flew open.

Her eyes were clear and green, the colour of water just beneath the sun-struck surface, and they were glittering with terror. They were the eyes of a fox, trapped, with the hounds closing in.

Maria drew a sharp breath. "Did you have a bad dream?"

Mrs. Cameron gave a queer, choked cry, and began to talk. Unintelligible words poured from her in a low, heart-broken voice. The rhythms and cadences of her own speech were there, and the lovely Celtic lilt, but it was only a babble, incomprehensible, grief-stricken, a measureless river flowing into a timeless sea. Perhaps she was speaking of some childhood sorrow or later loss, or of some bright image for ever extinguished, or perhaps it was a once-and-only protest against her imprisonment, a bitter cry of rebellion from a spirit resigned to bearing in dignity the extreme indignity of speechlessness, helplessness, the body's cruel betrayal of the spirit.

Finished, she wept, and so did Maria, her face against her mother's.

Across the room, Mrs. Preston wept too.

Then Mrs. Cameron recovered herself, indicated that she would get up. While she was in the bathroom with the nurse, and Maria was laying out her clothes, Mrs. Preston said, "Maria, I don't think you should take your poor mother out this evening. It's far too much for her."

"We have her doctor's permission." She added, with a fierceness that seemed directed at herself, "As long as she can *move*, we're going to keep her going."

"I admire your spirit. But you must think of her, too."

"Oh God," said Maria, under her breath.

Mrs. Cameron grimaced when she saw the wheel-chair Malcolm was pushing. "Oh...no," she said imploringly.

"Just this once, dear Mama," Maria said. "It's such a long journey to the door. Besides, you know I like pushing people around."

Mrs. Cameron laughed at that, and with a wave of her hand to Mrs. Preston, allowed herself to be wheeled away.

They brought Mrs. Cameron back before eight o'clock, and a nurse came immediately to help get her to bed. While she was occupied, Maria said to Mrs. Preston, "Would you mind if I sat with my mother this evening? She's not sick, just very tired. We wanted to keep her at home, but it seemed to worry her. I think she wanted to get back to her own room. And her room-mate," she added. "I would like to stay, and they said I must have your permission."

"Of course you have my permission! It won't bother me at all, I scarcely sleep anyway. I often envy your mother her sound sleep. Keep the light on, if you like, and read."

Malcolm said goodnight to his mother, and Maria walked down the hall with him. When she came back Mrs. Cameron was asleep, and Maria sat down and opened her book.

Later, Mrs. Cameron opened her eyes and gazed at Maria, who after a moment glanced up. She stood by the bed, taking her mother's hand, looking down at her.

Mrs. Cameron's eyes were luminous, and her face had an unearthly purity about it, as if fires had burned themselves out behind it, leaving only the last radiant embers.

"You're very beautiful, Mother," Maria said, in a wondering voice. "You have the face of a young boy, does that surprise you? You look like all your sons, when they were young. Is that the way you looked when Father first knew you?"

Mrs. Cameron made an effort to speak, breathing very fast. The pulse in her throat was fluttering.

"Don't try to talk." Maria bent over her. "I know what you want to say. That you love us all very much, isn't that it?" Tears trembled in her eyes, and in her voice.

Mrs. Cameron nodded, and smiled, peacefully. She drew Maria's hand to her face and held it there until her own relaxed in sleep. Maria put her mother's hand across her breast, where it lay like ivory against the crimson shawl. She kissed her mother's brow.

Sitting down again she began to read, and dozed off, and some time later wakened abruptly, as if something had pierced through her sleep. She leapt to her feet, and with a little gasp reached out and touched her mother's cold hand.

The staff was quiet and efficient, and Mrs. Preston did not know that anything had happened until she wakened in the morning and saw the empty bed. She rang her bell, and Mrs. McDermott came in and broke the news to her. Mrs. Preston was considerably upset. Mrs. McDermott suggested that she have her hair done when the beauty parlour opened at nine-thirty.

"Yes, I think the little change would do me good," Mrs. Preston said, drying her eyes.

When she was wheeled back, with her hair freshly done, Maria and Virginia and Flora were there. They had almost finished packing Mrs. Cameron's things, and loaded them on a trolley just outside the door. The pictures were gone from the walls, and the dresser was bare.

Mrs. Preston cried, holding Maria's hand. "You have the satisfaction of knowing you have been a devoted family," she said. "And your mother's time had come. I'm sure it was a merciful release for her."

"But not for us," Maria said. There were shadows under her eyes, and she was very pale. Turning, she said to Virginia in a slow sorrowful voice, "I've just realized that Malcolm and I are nobody's children any more. Isn't that a strange thing to mind, at forty-five?"

That was almost the only thing they said. Except that Virginia held up Mrs. Cameron's best dress, of heavy purple silk, and said, "Do you think this would be...."

Maria said quickly, "Please, you decide. I can't bear to think about it." She added, "I wish it could be a shroud."

Flora took the wigs from the box, and said, "Aunt Maria, which one do you think...."

Maria snatched the wigs from her, and stuffed them back in the box. "Neither! It would be an outrage." Flora's face crumpled, and Maria put her arms around her, and said, "Darling Flora, I didn't mean to be sharp. I only meant, I want her to be herself. Nothing false. You do understand?"

"Maria was certainly odd about the wig," Mrs. Preston said to Mrs. McDermott, who had come in to see how she was getting along. "Wouldn't you think she'd want her mother to look her best?"

"Perhaps she liked her best without," Mrs. McDermott said, checking dresser drawers to be sure nothing had been left behind.

"I'm certainly going to miss her. I always said she was a good companion, even though she couldn't talk, always so pleasant, and interested in everything. Of course in the last few weeks she got a bit queer. The brain was going, I suppose. Once she shook her cane at me. Maria was very upset, I could tell, so I passed it off as nothing. I gave Maria permission to stay last night. It was nice that she could be here when her mother went. She didn't thank me for it this morning. I suppose it slipped her mind." Mrs. Preston sighed. "I'm not looking forward to tonight, I can tell you, being all alone here, thinking about Mrs. Cameron going, just like that."

"Indeed, you're not going to be alone," Mrs. McDermott said, reassuringly. "Your new room-mate's arriving this afternoon, isn't that nice?"

"Goodness, this place is certainly in demand, isn't it." Mrs. Preston looked gratified.

"And you'll be ready with a nice cheery welcome, won't you. The maid will be in soon to freshen things up."

Mrs. Preston glanced about with a critical air. "While she's here, she can have another go at that spot. That's not very cheerful, is it!" She gave her little chuckle, and looked down at the carpet where a small stain, no bigger than a silver dollar, could still be faintly seen.

Counterpoint

"OH, WAS EVER ANYTHING SO DELICIOUS!" SOPHIA SPOONED *crème fraiche* onto her plate.

"It's almost more than I can bear, watching you eat those strawberries."

"Do have some." She pushed her plate towards him.

He shook his head. "I meant the way you eat them is so provocative. I must say, it's an unusual sight. You eating, that is. I've sometimes thought you'd starve to death."

She smiled at him, rolling a sweet berry on her tongue. "I like to eat. But when I'm having a lovely time I'm inclined to lose my appetite."

"It's rather a nice trait. It can be off-putting, watching a woman eat. One can take an absolutely heavenly woman to lunch, with all sorts of high expectations for the afternoon, and there she suddenly is, stoking away. One's inclined to remember a pressing engagement for three o'clock. That can never have happened to you, can it."

"If it has, I haven't known. I don't make love with every man who takes me to lunch. Usually I just go home and practise."

"Do you indeed?" He raised an eyebrow, smiling. "Thank God there isn't a piano handy."

"Anyway, this is dinner."

"True. More coffee? No? Then shall we go somewhere else for a Calvados?"

The proprietor, with the grave demeanour of a surgeon in consultation, wished them a good evening and bowed them out. It was clear from his manner that Nicholas was a respected patron.

Stepping outside, Sophia was for a moment disoriented. There was the river, tracked with silver, but she was not certain whether they were on the Left Bank or the Right. It did not matter. Paris, to her, was Nicholas.

He took her arm just above the elbow in a grip possessive and protective. She liked that. She was infatuated with his total style: the loose-limbed tallness, the English fairness and fine voice, his immaculate tailoring, his understated ease with everything — money, language, customs, waiters, all the niceties of discreet arrangements.

An old man in a cap was selling newspapers in a kiosk lighted by a street lamp. They slowed their steps, glancing at the headlines. A London paper announced that the British had occupied I.R.A. strongholds in Belfast.

"It's not over yet," Nicholas said. "Not by a long shot. What a bloody business."

"For both sides," she said, mildly. He was pro-British, she pro-I.R.A. He was pro-Arab, she, like her Jewish husband, pro-Israel. He had been a hawk on Vietnam, she a dove. It was not for his political or sociological opinions that she was in love with him. She was in love despite them.

He said, in a lighter voice, "We'll go to the Ritz, shall we, and pay our respects to the literary past of your country?"

"I don't see any budding Hemingways or Fitzgeralds here, do you?" She did see, with a start of surprise and delight, that the vivid-looking woman across the room was herself, reflected in a long looking-glass. A party of Americans had established themselves at a table nearby, middle aged, loud voiced, prosperous, the women with metallic hair, and arms jangling with bracelets. Their brassy confidence jarred Sophia. She had been in Rome for six months — her husband, a pianist turned composer, had a fellowship at the American Academy — and with their two small children they lived in an apartment just off Via Giulia. Only on an occasional expedition along the Via Veneto had she come upon such Americans-abroad. "They're like sharp objects in a hardware store, those women."

"True of most American women."

"You know the wrong sort. I have women friends who are marvellous."

"I should like to meet the other sort." He sounded dubious. "The fact is you're the only American woman I've ever wanted to make love with."

She heard the slight stress on "wanted". "In most cases, you just grit your teeth and go to it?"

"I have a strong sense of duty. To myself, at least."

Did she, by her own cheap, tough remarks, force that kind of response from him? In the beginning she had assumed that he was as much in love as she was, and had been badly jolted — though careful never to betray it — by his ever-ready fund of stories about other women, past and present. Quickly she had learned to match her nonchalance to his, having taken her cue from an anecdote related at their first lunch together, at Quo Vadis. It was about a "ravishing" girl who, half-undressed, had suddenly said in a conscience-stricken voice, But Nicholas, I don't know if I really love you. And had put her clothes back on. Sophia had laughed, of course — ho-ho to a girl, however ravishing, with such absurd scruples — knowing full well that she was laughing at herself. Often enough she had said the same thing, though admittedly not in a state of undress: that, conceivably, made the story amusing. She had understood it as a warning: This is the way we play the game — remember, it is only a game. Knowing that, she had still chosen to play. Now she realized that it had been a little morality, Nicholas's little, icy morality. She returned her attention to what he was saying.

"...gaga by the end of that month Mary and the children and I spent in Newport. Not one lovely woman. Lots of spectacular twenty-year-olds, but I'm not interested in the cradle. So when you appeared in that extraordinary house — how those robber barons loved to get their houses up! — I could hardly believe my eyes."

"Or your ears, I hope. After all, I did play that evening."

"Elliott Carter. You see I did listen, as well as look. That russet hair falling across your face, and the way you smiled at your partner before each movement. I was green with envy. And considerably dashed, consulting the program, to learn that you were married to the romantic-looking young man who played so brilliantly. I resented his playing first piano, as I had to crane my head to look at you. Your arms, the way you moved on that black padded seat, sent all sorts of speculations chasing through my mind."

"A critic in Los Angeles once wrote, nastily, that he didn't know which to admire more, my dancing or my playing."

"What a churl. You were too sexy for him, I expect. That displeases you? Do you think music should be pure of sex?"

"I think I should be, playing. Music can be very sexual. I'm not thinking of Wagner's tumescent harmonies — there are certain preludes of Bach's, for instance, that I feel myself in love with. I have to be restrained, I might float away. I'm thinking of the E-flat minor. Do you know it? So beautiful — a saraband. I have a passion for sarabands. I wish I'd lived when they were danced. It goes like this." Her head close to his, she sang softly, repeated a long ascending line. "Did you hear that, the C-natural that's so unexpected? It's electrifying."

"It is, as you sing it. Perhaps I should come to Rome and study piano with you. My knowledge of music is sadly deficient. Would you be willing to take on an aging, untalented student?"

"Hard work is all I ask."

"I would make every effort, for you."

They smiled at each other, willing themselves not to touch. In a moment he went on. "I shall never forget your playing, that evening. I applauded so heartily that my hostess said, 'Why Nicholas, I thought you weren't fond of music.' It was obtuse of her to confuse my balking at being dragged to a benefit concert on a hot summer night with my not liking music. I said, I always applaud a charming musician. Whereupon she — rather maliciously — said, 'Oho, typical Nicholas. It's that girl you like.'"

Sophia knew exactly the tone in which "that girl" had

been said. Musician = paid performer = servant. She took a momentary pleasure in hating him for repeating it, for speaking of her as a "charming musician". Hating him, she despised herself too, and had a sudden withering glimpse of herself as his occasional paramour, rushing to be with him at his bidding in Munich, in New York, in Paris, pretending it was all incidental, that like the other women in his life her body's ardour left her Lucite heart untouched, that love had nothing at all to do with love-making. Wasn't she, in her "real" life, a hundred times better than any of those unnamed women who flashed their cool fire through his amorous recollections? But how could he know, when she had taken such pains to hide from him what she really was? And immediately she softened towards him, watching him, listening to him reminisce about that first evening. It was flattering, it was thrilling, that his memory was so detailed: did it matter if he had recollections as seductively vivid for twenty women? Or a hundred?

He was quoting his Newport hostess. "'... shall I tell Mary that you do want, after all, to go on to the party after the concert?' she asked me. I said, by all means, and all the time I was watching you. You were smiling as you took your bows, trying, I thought, not to laugh. I wondered what at? Possibly at the audience. It was tantalizing—I longed to make you laugh. Which I did, on a later occasion. Our first together. Do you remember?"

"Yes, I do," she said, on a little sigh.

"And who is making you laugh these days?"

"The cast of the *Commedia dell'Arte*."

"No, seriously, Sophia. You've been very reticent. I'm

certain you're keeping something back. What about the sculptor you spoke of, in Munich?"

"I said I liked his work. And yes, I like him."

"Much more than that, I'd say. All those expeditions to look at Etruscan tomb-paintings, and cosy family weekends in Tuscany."

"You ask so many questions, and then you jump to conclusions." She supposed that his liking to make her talk about "other men" was his idea of fair play: he had mistresses, she must have lovers. She could not tell him that since meeting him she had had no other lover, and had wanted no other. That would frighten him — the idea of her being "faithful" to him. He would see it as entangling. It seemed sad to her that after two years he did not trust her to be as undemanding as he wanted her to be.

"Natural enough, surely?"

She tipped the brandy around in her glass. There was a half-moon of light in its dark gleaming.

"He is your lover, isn't he. You're thinking about him, now."

She dismissed the impression she had had of a note of anxiety in his voice, and said, lightly, "You'd never believe, would you, that with most men I'm just friends."

"No man in his right mind would be content to have you just as a friend."

She saw for the first time, with surprise and an odd kind of pity, that he was limited, not liberated, by his voracious sexuality. For surely in *philios* there were joys and satisfactions more enduring than those of *eros*? As if her thought had been spoken, he said, "Though I do like to think of you as my friend, quite apart from anything else."

His desolate tone struck a little blow at her heart. "You must know that I am." Some inner struggle was reflected in his face, and she had — not for the first time — the sense of his being on the edge of some unspeaking unreachable despair. She longed to help him, but did not know how. Where no love was admitted, and no trust was implicit, how could one help? She thought of saying, I'm here, we can talk. You don't have to make love to me. I wouldn't be let down, I wouldn't think the less of you, I love you.

But two years of guarding herself had made such a speech impossible. Instead she said, "The woman across the room who looks like a Lely portrait — is that a dog she's carrying, or a fur muff?"

His face recovered, as if on cue. "I think a dog. I distinctly heard a yap a while ago. You're quite right — she might have been one of Charles the Second's beauties. Those drowsy-eyed languid ladies are not at all to my taste."

"In life or in portraits?"

"In neither."

They talked on, about pictures and about other people in the room which was by now crowded, mainly with Americans.

"Shall we be off? But first, if you'll excuse me, I'll make a telephone call."

Watching him return, confident, so enormously attractive, she laughed aloud for the sheer pleasure of seeing him.

"Fate smiles on us," he said. "I thought for our last night we might have a change from that hotel room, much as I have enjoyed it."

In the Place Vendôme they took a taxi. Inside, he turned to her, his arm stretched along the back of the seat, his fingers just touching her bare arm. Her knees were glossed by street-lights. He touched her throat. "What a lovely pulse."

"Is it a long drive?" she whispered.

"No." He kissed her. "What a lovely mouth. You're radiating heat, like a beautiful furnace."

The taxi drew up in front of a tall sombre-looking house. No light came through the heavily curtained windows on the ground floor. Nicholas lifted the door-knocker — a bronze hand — and a woman admitted them. She was dressed in black silk and had a long stony face. They walked down a carpeted hall into a small room. One wall was lined with books. On tables there were lamps with fringed shades, and a few petals had fallen from a bowl of roses to a polished table. The woman said something, and Nicholas with a small bow excused himself and followed the woman out of the room. Sophia picked up a *Paris Match* and glanced through it: colours of pictures and chunks of print leaped from the pages. She felt intensely alive, she felt brilliant and beautiful. Nicholas did that for her.

He came back, and said, "We can only stay until five o'clock. It's midnight now. Shall you mind having to leave so early?"

She shook her head.

They went up a wide curving staircase, footsteps muffled by thick carpeting. Opening a door, the woman flicked a glance over Sophia's face, as sharp as a whip-lash. Disturbed by that look, Sophia said, "What an unusual hotel." An immense bed stood in the centre of the room, covers turned back to show hemstitched sheets. On an ornately carved table there was a bowl of roses, wine-dark in the lamplight. She bent her head to their heavy sweetness. Nicholas put his watch on the table. He had taken off his jacket, and was loosening his tie. She wandered into the bathroom. "This must be the biggest tub in Paris." On the marble washstand there was bath-powder, a very clean brush and comb, a bottle of *Ma Griffe* toilet water, and a packet of papers for removing lipstick. "It's not like any hotel I've ever seen."

He smiled. "I'm not sorry to hear that. It's a *maison particulière*. Are you shocked?"

She did not say she had never heard of a *maison particulière*.

She drew a long breath, stretching her arms high above her head, and bringing them down again to rest on his head.

"What a lovely tidal wave that was," he said contentedly. "Speaking of which, it's a pity, isn't it, that so much of the time there's an ocean between us."

"Perhaps it's a good thing." She was thinking — without that ocean he would feel unprotected.

"You'd find me boring? Too demanding?"

"Neither of those."

"You don't like involvements. You told me that, long ago. You said you'd resolved to have nothing serious outside your marriage."

"Which suited you to a T," she quickly said.

"I suppose it did."

"It's what's nice about our friendship. We have a good

time when we meet, and no moping between. In my experience, men are the possessive ones. They always start by saying 'nothing serious' and then, so quickly, become serious, then unhappy, then difficult. I couldn't manage before, all the time trying to be a good wife and mother too, and some sort of musician. I felt I had plenty of love to go round, but not enough me. I couldn't be responsible for so many people, it tore me apart." That was spoken in truth—but it was pride, the necessity to defend her *amour propre* against the one lover who had not become serious, who had never said he loved her, that made her add, "What a relief you are, just wanting fun."

He looked at her speculatively, as if about to say something, then changed his mind. After a moment, he said, "It's usually true, though, that it's the woman who's possessive, wanting to put a man in a cage. Tempted by the bird inside, he slips in, and bang, the door slams shut. And somehow, no matter how honeyed and scented the cage, restlessness sets in, the golden bars become prison bars. In fact, I've just recently escaped from such a cage, with considerable distress."

"Poor, poor Nicholas! My heart bleeds for you."

"I suppose I deserved that." He was silent a moment. "But you're quite right, it's impossible to work, get anything done. What a winter! Act 1. Scenes with a jealous mistress. Act 2. Scenes with a —justifiably—angry wife. Act. 3. Nicholas the Penitent, trotting docilely off to balls and dinners and country weekends, and to the children's school for gymkhanas and lamentable theatricals, and playing, at home, the ever-genial husband and host. Except for that delicious fling you gave me in Munich, it's

73

been a ghastly winter. And all the time that loathsome book to haunt me."

"You were writing it when I first met you."

"Oh God, don't remind me. Don't let's talk about it."

Some waywardness, unbidden, seized her. "I want to talk about it. It's important, isn't it? You told me you were coming to Paris to finish it."

"That's what I told Mary, and the publisher who's being surly about deadlines. I told him I wanted to give a little more time to Ledoux. If I told you anything of the sort, it was to entice you here. I didn't want to put in writing that I was coming only to see you and be revived. You'd have thought that a dreadful responsibility, wouldn't you."

"No, I wouldn't." She deliberated, looking at the roses. Then said, boldly but at the same time soberly, "Why do you put up with it? Why do you make your life such a . . . carnival?"

"Weak-mindedness."

"You're not weak-minded. You're undisciplined. Couldn't you determine to do nothing but the book until it's done? Even if it meant giving up women? I don't mean to be harsh about that — especially at this moment — but it would help, wouldn't it?" (Would he think she was trying to imprison him in her cage?) "No distractions, no guilt, no atonement-through-more-time-wasting. . . ."

"And no fun."

"Oh, fun!" She didn't try to disguise her contempt.

"I'm quoting you, my love. 'What a relief you are, just wanting fun.'"

"You make me talk like that! I do it to please you. I'm afraid of. . . ." She stopped herself.

"What are you afraid of?"

"Of offending you, by being serious. So I can never tell you what I think — or talk to you."

"About me? Please do. I am eager to know." His voice glinted.

She looked at him, considering, resolving not to speak of love, the forbidden topic. Still, a certain recklessness possessed her. She said, "All right. We'll never agree about politics. That's understood. Perhaps history will prove you right, and me wrong. But I wish you *cared*. Isn't there anything you want to do with your life? There must be something! Something that you're using the book to keep you from doing, as you use your friends to keep you from the book?"

After a moment, he said, "I'd like to make one good building. The kind that people like you would look at and say, You see? If he hadn't been such a fool he might have amounted to something. But I'll go on grinding out stuff about what other people are doing — and being on BBC panels, sounding astute about urban planning, and earnest about the housing problems of the aged and the under-privileged and ne'er-do-wells. I'll take another look at the Barbican, as requested, and say it's even worse than I thought: a glass and steel rabbit-warren for people who deserve exactly that —— "

She burst in, "I can't bear to hear you talk like that! 'A rabbit warren for people who deserve exactly that.' That sickens me. You were born fortunate. You're in a position to do such good things. . . . "

"Indeed I am. Let's make the most of it."

"No, don't." She pushed away his caressing hand. "It makes me angry that you waste your time and talent. And dissipate your energy, chasing after...." She stopped, and sat up suddenly, pulling the sheet up over her breasts.

"What an inappropriate time for a lecture." He turned on his back, looking up at the garlanded nymphs and cupids at play on the ceiling.

"No, don't you see? I'm angry with myself, too. I'm as bad for you as all the others you talk about with their gilded scented cages. I've let you throw away days, I've let you break appointments, I've even — I just now realize — enjoyed knowing one man to whom women are more important than accomplishing something."

"A pretty picture you paint of me. I shall soon be the old goat in a comic opera."

"Oh, *no!*" In her turn, she was stung by the picture he had painted. "Don't you see, if I really...."

He grasped her wrist. "Really what?"

"Oh — loved you, cared about you, whatever the word is that you so dislike, I wouldn't have let you waste all that time on me."

He let go of her wrist, and turned away with a sigh. "Nothing could ever be wasted on you."

"That's very sweet of you." She touched his shoulder.

"I suppose you're used to people who have huge ambitions."

"Is that contemptible?"

"On the contrary." He became elaborately polite. "You know, it's a new experience for me, being ticked off in bed like this. For other reasons, yes, but never, I swear, have I been scolded for not caring enough about God's poor." He paused. "Perhaps in time it will seem to have been rather a droll episode."

"Perhaps it will." She heard it, a small narrative entertainment for his next encounter. ". . . I found myself in bed with an American pianist, very pretty, and capable, I must admit, of superb performance. But like so many Americans she had no sense of occasion, and just as we were settling down for a nice talk she started up a clatter about my short-comings as a humanitarian, of all unlikely things. . . ." Stop, she cried silently to herself, and aloud she said, "I'm sorry. I've finished."

Pain at her loss mingled with humiliation at being so summarily rejected, and lay like a weight on her heart. To have ended their pleasurings like this! She was a mere episode in his *concerto grosso*, why had she tried to play a larger part? But it was done, it was said, she could not, would not try with cajolery to restore his interest in her. She would pretend nothing had happened, at least she would salvage her pride. Stubborn and proud, she sat against the pillows. His eyes were closed, his arms folded across his breast. She saw her clothes lying in a heap on the floor. Was that *her* — the gaudy Pucci bra and slip, the black linen dress? The roses throbbed in their pool of light; she looked away, wounded by them. Somewhere, in another room, a woman coughed, a dry, desolate sound, infinitely melancholy.

Out of the silence, he said vehemently, "I should never have brought you to this bloody place."

"I've liked it." But she heard her voice tremble in its bravado, and decided to get up before she burst into tears. He caught her arm as she moved, and in a quick motion sat up. "Where are you going?"

"To try out that mammoth tub."

"What a waste of time. And we have so little left."

"I'll be quick."

"Wait a minute." Still holding her arm, he said, "Would you believe me if I said that I'm going to finish the book, this month?"

She saw the book, finished, in a bookshop window, his picture on the dust-jacket, saw herself staring at it through the glass. "Yes," she said. But it no longer mattered that the book be finished. So were they.

There was a long looking-glass in the bathroom, and she could see him in it, dressing. The speed with which he dressed, his immediate, immaculate look was something she had always noticed: what evidence it was of his having dressed, a thousand times, with the clock pursuing him — a husband returning, a "pressing engagement" to be met, his hour up. He came to the door, watching her, as she briskly towelled herself.

"How beautiful you are." He put his hands on her breasts. "We'd have had three more hours if we'd gone to the hotel."

Something — was it his saying that? — lifted her spirit. "But I've loved this. I wouldn't have missed it for anything."

He waited for her, stretched out in a deep chair, long legs sprawling. Rising, he handed her the Hermés scarf and the fine white kid gloves he had given her that morning. She drew the gloves on, and going downstairs was aware of the gesture as absurdly inappropriate. Such propriety. She smiled, thinking about it, and seeing the woman at the foot of the stairs, smiled at her too, straight into the flinty face, and said, "*Buon giorno, Signora*." Behind the woman, the library door was closed. Another couple would be waiting there.

The woman led them down the hall, her back stiff, keys jingling on the chain she carried. She let them out into the cool, silver morning. A taxi waited at the curb.

"It's all very efficient, isn't it?" she said, conversationally. "Do you suppose someone else is hopping into that bed now? Though I suppose it would take a few minutes to change the sheets."

"Please," he said, wincing.

She felt rebuked, guilty of a vulgarism. They drove along in silence.

"Could we get out and walk?" she asked. "It's such a lovely morning."

They were at the Pont des Arcs. The spires of Notre Dame rose against the sky in which a few coral-coloured clouds drifted. The river, still as glass, reflected trees and houses and dawn sky. Downstream, the Louvre gleamed in the calm light. That inexplicable buoyancy of spirit remained with her, and she was grateful to it, as she was to the morning for being fair and tranquil. The loss of a lover who had never loved her could be borne.

He leaned on the bridge, beside her. "What are you thinking?"

She countered. "What are you thinking?"

"That I've lost you for ever."

That confused her. Did he then greatly mind?

"Your turn," he said.

"I was thinking it's all been a great lark." She was

pleased by her tone. He liked lightness; he would know
that her seriousness had been a passing mood. Tiresome
for him, but over, and unimportant.

"It's been more than a lark, hasn't it?"

She looked down into the water. On the almost imper-
ceptible current a branch was slowly moving. What did he
want her to say, what did he want to draw out of her, now
that it was too late? Now that it was over, did he want the
satisfaction of knowing that for her it had been real, an
honest-to-God love affair? He with his sense of love as a
trap, his fear of it! As she wondered what to say her voice
spoke for her. "From our apartment in Rome, we look
down on the Tiber. Every morning a little sky-blue row-
boat goes down the river, under the Ponte Umberto,
under the Ponte Cavour, with a man in it, fishing. I've
never seen him catch anything, and I've never seen him
come back up. He just goes down, every morning."

Nicholas straightened up, a sudden shaft of sunlight
gilding his fair hair. He seemed not to have heard her.

She said matter-of-factly, "I suppose we should get
back to the hotel. My plane leaves at eleven, and I have to
pack, and pick up presents for the children, and —— "

"Then for you, it has been just a lark."

She heard again in his tone, glimpsed in his tightened,
tired face, the desperation — the cause of which after two
years she still did not understand — that drove him along,
ruthless in his treatment of himself and of others, as
acquisitive of women as if they had been *bibelots* for a
collection. Alarmed by love, he lived in a cage of his own
making, which she, for one, would gladly have shared had

he permitted it. Putting aside pride and pretence, she said, gently, "No. It's been much, much more than that."

"You're sure?" His voice pounced at her.

"Nicholas, don't you *know*?" she cried.

"I never know, with you."

She saw — and felt as a blow — how well she had played his game. She said, "Well, now you do," and smiled at him — and heard how light and careless her tone sounded, how, despite herself, she continued the game.

"What a tease you are, Sophia." His face took on again its handsome armour, his voice that seductive confidence. In a gesture rare for him — he never touched her in public — he bent and kissed her, and took her hand in his. "When shall I see you again? Can I tempt you to England?"

"We're thinking of Edinburgh, for the Festival."

"I begin to feel rather drawn to Edinburgh myself. Though not precisely for the Festival. Would you be there the entire time? We might — if your calendar permits — take a run to Inverness-shire. Handsome country." He added, in his characteristic way, "Did I ever tell you? It's a county that has romantic associations for me."

"Has it indeed?" She gave him a sideways glance, pretending conspiratorial amusement, and hand in hand they began to walk, going nowhere, walking across the bridge which seemed to float as in a dream above the motionless river.

Tales from a *pensione*

"...IF I'D STAYED WITH FRIENDS," SHE WAS SAYING, "I couldn't have kept my days to myself, for looking. And I don't like hotels when I'm on my own—they make me feel like an abandoned woman. In its way, that *pensione* pleased me. It was like finding myself in a novel by...."

"Vicki Baum," he put in.

"Goodness, could you have heard of her? No, it wasn't like that at all, no high crime or passion, and only a very faded grandeur. But thoroughly familiar, I knew it as if I'd been there before; the worn marble staircase, the velvet draperies and busts of J. Caesar and N. Machiavelli, the roaring plumbing, old steamer trunks in the hall and Piranesi prints and water-colour sketches of Tuscan hills hung too high to be properly seen. And the view, from my balcony, of the Boboli gardens. Nothing could have changed there in fifty years. Except for the television set sputtering away in a reception room. The old grand-mother sat in front of it all day long, knitting on something grey and thick, like herself."

He got up, stretching, and crossed the room to stand at

the sliding glass doors that opened out on a terrace. A wooded valley dropped away beneath, and over the distant hills clouds were gathering, muting the brilliance of the autumn foliage. His clothes — a faded fisherman's shirt, torn around the neck, and baggy blue jeans — sagged around his gaunt body. He wore shabby work boots, laced up with bits of cord and string. His brown hair fell in heavy tangles to his shoulders.

"Do you feel like a cup of tea?"

"I've never felt like a cup of tea." He wandered out of the room.

Sitting at her desk — she had been writing letters — one arm resting on the desk, the other dangling over the back of the chair, she appeared to be studying the chair he had just vacated. Her hair, unbound, and on this damp day crinkly, was a darkening gold that emphasized the pallor of her skin. One noticed her long neck, well-defined jaw and high cheek-bones, most of all her eyes, which were oval in shape and the colour of amber. She seemed not exactly relaxed, but relieved to put aside for a moment her customary animation.

The room in which she sat was even on this dull day full of colour — of flowers, paintings, fabrics, book-bindings. There was about it all a blend of sophistication and simplicity that spoke of a taste not primarily expensive, but highly individual, highly assured.

"Oh, good," she exclaimed when he came back. "You found the ginger-beer. I was hiding it."

"I know you were."

"Not *from* you. For you. Did you think to put the kettle on?"

"No, I didn't think to put the kettle on."

Sitting down, he propped his feet on the table in front of him, pushing aside with the heel of his boot a bowl of pink and purple asters. Some of the water spilled on the polished table-top and she got up and not fussily but with a kind of abstracted air wiped away the drops of water with the palm of her hand. He watched her, a shade of disdain in his eyes which were so like hers. His face was modelled on hers, and in the waning light they might have passed for brother and older sister.

Straightening up, she said, "I ought to be doing something about dinner. Will you..." she hesitated, then added, "be having dinner with us?"

"I don't know. I haven't decided."

"Well, let me know soon. It's full *pensione* here, but we like to know in advance how many of our guests will be dining." She smiled at him, tentatively, as if hoping for but not expecting a smile in response. Her attitude was that of a hostess eager to please an unusually difficult guest, one who for reasons not immediately apparent must be treated with delicacy.

"Tell me more about the pension." Pronouncing it that way seemed to amuse him. At least he smiled, faintly.

"Do you really want to know? That's so nice of you!" She sat opposite him, stretching out her legs, crossing her ankles. She wore well-cut trousers, and a long sweater, belted, and buttoned high at the throat. "The proprietor was Giuseppi. A sleek young man, immensely polite though managing at the same time to be rather disagreeable...."

"True, usually, of 'polite' people."

"That's debatable," she said, "but let's not. His wife had just had a baby. They named it Antonia. I wish I'd thought of Antonia. Too late now. Giuseppi's mother was rather formidable — horrible to the maids, and touchy about keys. I suppose I deserved it, I was always losing mine, as usual. Good looking, though, with masses of glossy black hair and a splendid nose. Her husband was called Dante. He carried bags and called taxis and fixed things. Sort of. One day he tied two ladders together with rope, to make one long ladder. Can you imagine anything more disastrous?"

"Did disaster result?" As she talked, he had been blowing lightly across the mouth of his empty bottle, producing a series of crescendos and de-crescendos. His eyes were expressionless.

"No, because when he propped the ladder up and climbed the bottom one it dawned on him that his fix wouldn't do. He made some indignant muttering, coming down, laid the ladder out on the sidewalk for people to fall over, and hopped off to the corner bar."

"Why did he hop? Is he one-legged?"

"Well — walked."

"A verb should describe an action, not distort it."

"Right you are." She nodded, apparently pleased by his correction, as if she took it as an indication that he had, after all, some proprietary interest in her. "From now on, no fooling around with verbs." She lit a cigarette, caught his look, and said, "I know it's a dirty, unhealthy, expensive habit, but they're my lungs."

"It's my air you're polluting."

She started to put the cigarette out, had second

thoughts about it. "How gloomy it is, all at once." She got up, touched a wall switch, and pin-points of light appeared in the ceiling. "Shall we have a fire?"

"I'm warm enough."

"Oh — then I am, too."

He yawned. "Go on about the pension."

"I don't think you really want to hear, why should you? It's all very dull. Maybe I'll make a drink." She crossed the room with a rapid step, bouncing a fraction on her heels, as if being in motion exhilarated her. She opened a pair of doors set into a wall, on which there was a *trompe l'oeil* painting of books on shelves, some standing, some tilted, some lying on their sides. Inside the cupboard were bottles and glasses. She poured vermouth into a glass, added a few drops of cassis, and sitting down again, said, "Like the place itself, the people were absolutely familiar, so predictable that they came as a surprise. Do you know what I mean? There actually *was* a contessa whose family — like the Bastables — suffered from fallen fortunes, and there were two Browning scholars, refined American lady-teachers, who spent their days at Casa Guidi rummaging through old letters and laundry bills, hoping to turn up some thrilling new fact about their hero. I quite liked them. Except that they always had the 'sniffles' and carried boxes of 'tissues' wherever they went. And another aging widow, this one English, always elegantly turned out as if for a fashionable lunch party though she never to my knowledge left the *pensione*. A hairdresser and a manicurist waited on her twice a week, and twice a day a woman came to walk her dog. She had a daughter who drove down from Milan, called her Darling Mummy about sixty-five times in twenty minutes and then left, saying she'd be back in two weeks for another nice visit. Her Italian lover was lurking in the lounge, flashing his smile about. The dog was a Pekinese. One day he sneaked into my room from the balcony and peed against the table leg. He yapped every morning from three o'clock until six. Maddening, as her room was next to mine."

"Did you complain to the management?"

She drew in her brows in a way she had, and said, "Oh, no! The dog was all she had, poor old thing."

"You complain plenty when Butterfly howls at night."

The old beagle, who had been dozing on the hearth, lifted her head, and getting up padded laboriously across the room. "Sweet ol' Butterfly, ol' dum-dums, ol' silly girl...." He went on crooning endearments, picking the dog up and putting her on the sofa beside him.

"Please don't put..." she began, and stopped.

He settled the dog to his satisfaction, her head on a cushion embroidered in a Celtic design. "And besides the old lady who was neglected by her thankless child?"

She looked at him, uneasily, and away again. "I don't think you like my little anecdotes. I don't blame you. Travel talk is deadly dull."

"Why do you keep saying it's dull?"

She shrugged. "I suppose because you convey so clearly that it is."

"By asking questions?"

"*Touché*." She attempted a laugh and, effort audible in her voice, started in again. "There was a gargantuan couple from Waltham, Mass., who yearned every morning for a *real* breakfast, of hot-cakes and maple syrup. Every time I saw them they were chomping on something."

"Eating is disgusting. I've often told you that. Forkfuls

of murdered animals, squished up roots and leaves." His words, as always, were well enunciated, his voice low pitched, fine in quality, but in intonation flat, indifferent.

"*Eating* isn't disgusting, it's being obsessed by it. And you should eat, you're skin and bone, I worry about you, it could be dangerous. . . . " She hurried on, as if she feared to offend him by showing concern for him. "They were also disappointed in Florence because there weren't any bargains. Typical."

"Of what?"

"Of middle-aged American tourists."

"You were one, weren't you?"

She laughed. "Yes, but I like to think not typical. It's odd, but I don't feel middle aged. Except when I wear sensible shoes. I bought a pair, but I gave them away. They made me feel dowdy."

"Who was the lucky recipient?"

"A young art-history student, from California. She was there on a grant. I didn't much like her, but I felt sorry for her. She was lonely, though she didn't admit it. She'd say grudgingly, 'If you're going to the Carmine, I might as well come along.' Or, 'What train are you taking to Arezzo, I might as well go today.' Not exactly winning. On the other hand, she was a first-rate guide, she knew where everything was — there were things I'd have missed without her — and she had every story and legend on the tip of her tongue. Very handy. Her special interest was borders in *trecento* fresco painting. That speaks volumes, doesn't it."

"It doesn't say a word to me."

"Oh, come on! It's like being interested in the frame, rather than the painting. Though I suppose frames are

interesting to a frame-maker. And the borders were intriguing, once I'd begun to look at them."

"So what volumes were spoken by her interest in
them?"

She said thoughtfully, "It suggested that she was a step
removed from life. From fear of it, not from deep spiritual-
ity. She didn't look afraid, she looked arrogant. She was
handsome, with good legs and teeth and hair, and that
uncluttered California style. But how cold she was, and
ungiving! She could scarcely part with a smile, and she
gave ten-lire tips, and stepped over beggars as if they
didn't exist. She was divorced, with a child she hadn't seen
in five years. That would account for it, wouldn't it, for the
coldness. Or vice versa. She was an ardent Nixonite, said
he'd been 'crucified' by the American public. You can see
we hadn't much in common. She had a way of staring at
one, unblinking, that always made me babble on. And all at
once she'd take a little jab."

"Such as?"

"About my going out to dinner every evening — if I
knew that many people in Florence why was I staying in a
pensione, or what was I all 'gussied-up' for, was I going to a
ball with the Medicis. Deflating. And once, when we were
talking about population growth and what was to be done
about it, she said with a little scornful smile, 'If you don't
mind my saying so, Elizabeth, as the mother of six children
you're scarcely qualified to sound off on that subject.'"

"She was right, wasn't she?"

"Julian, she was talking about living people! She could
have meant *you*. Doesn't it seem a trifle officious for her to
suggest that you shouldn't exist? I told her that ours was a

different generation, and that if we'd seen — your father and I — how the world was going, we probably wouldn't have. . . ." She stopped, seeing his smile.

"Which ones of us wouldn't you have had?"

"All right." She leaned forward, fiddling with a small sculpture piece on the table, an abstract shape in gleaming bronze, rising from a black base. "But I think you know what I mean. Of course once a child is born you can't possibly imagine life without that child. How could I possibly say of any of you — except Peter — aha, I should have stopped there? In the fifties and early sixties I suppose we were somewhat hazy about our responsibilities, not to our children, but to the future of the world we live in, the very air we breathe. It's different for your generation. Two will probably be the decent limit, self-imposed. . . ."

A door banged, and a boy of about ten burst into the room. Fair haired, blue eyed, he still had about his face an appealing softness. On the front of his muddy sweatshirt was stamped Peter the Great. Breathless, he said, "Listen, can Christie spend the night here? His parents are away and they've got this finky baby-sitter he can't stand and she said gladly he could stay. So is it all right, we're going out to work on the fort, we have to winterize it."

"Fine." She reached out and caught his grubby hand in hers. "Just remember it's a school night, so don't ask for a look at the idiot box. Agreed?"

"Agreed." He leaned over the back of her chair, dropped a kiss on top of her head. "Good old Moms!" To Julian, he said, "See you later, Alligator."

Julian ignored him.

She said quickly, "After a while, Crocodile," and looked

after him fondly, as he went whistling away. Putting a hand to her hair she said, "I think he left a dribble of bubble-gum behind," and added, with a mock sigh, "Oh, the flown years! It's no time since I was Sheba, golden-haired queen of the jungle, and now I'm good old Moms."

"You asked for it."

"I don't regret it. A passing thought, that's all. It amused me."

He eyed her, dispassionately. "You haven't changed much, in the flown years."

"How nice of you!" Obviously pleased, she glanced at him. Then said, dubiously, "Or was it? Perhaps you meant that I should have changed? If only I could have changed for the better." Her eyes were suddenly full of tears, and she put her hands to her face to hide them.

He got up. "I think I'll get some more of that saucy ginger-beer."

She rose too, and going to the glass doors that led to the terrace, stood looking out into the gathering darkness. It had begun to rain. After a moment she turned, and surveyed the room, tapping her foot to the beat of the music that sounded from upstairs, a well-worn Beatles record. Julian, returning, sang along with it, "I can get by with a little help from my friends...." There was a tone of youthful purity in his baritone voice, and looking at him, her eyes were tender.

"You need a little help from your cobbler," she said, as he propped his feet up on the table. "You have a hole in your sole."

He drew on his ginger-beer.

"It wasn't a criticism. Just a comment."

"A comment implies a criticism, doesn't it? Pro or con. What you meant was, my boots displease you. You think I should get them mended."

"Oh dear. Yes, I suppose I did. That is, I was offering to get them mended."

"I don't want them mended."

"Then that's settled, isn't it."

"I hope so."

She lifted her ·head, started to speak, stopped, tried again. "Why do you make — why do we make..." she corrected herself carefully, "an issue of such things? To mend, or not to mend, a pair of boots. It's deadening. And we were having such a nice conversation. At least, I was." She attempted a smile. "I was just getting to the finish."

"Here's to the finish." He lifted his bottle, as if in a toast.

She said nothing, did not look at him. Tense, she sat on the edge of her chair as if ready to spring up, be off at the slightest signal.

"I meant, I'm waiting to hear it." He hunched his shoulders, frowning.

"It's nothing much," she said. "I don't know why I thought you'd be interested. It was just a mother and son, travelling together. I thought she was his grandmother, and almost said so. What a *gaffe* that would have been." As she talked, her voice took on its earlier sparkle. "The son was very attractive...."

"Did he have short hair and well-polished loafers?"

She said, good-naturedly, "Long hair, and a beard — all very shining and well-combed. He wore army fatigues, neatly pressed — perhaps he put them under his mattress — and army boots. He reminded me a little of you."

"I don't see how. All that well-combed shining."

"But his voice was low and pleasant, and his glance was direct. He must have been about your age. He'd just graduated from one of those Long Island colleges — the Italian tour was his widowed mother's graduation present to him. They were sharing a room, which struck me as... well, awkward."

He assumed a blank look, then said, "An economy, I suppose."

"Yes, obviously. But if I'd been in his shoes... I mean, can you imagine my asking Jake, or even Peter, to share a room with me? Let alone...."

"Let alone me."

Colour rose in her cheeks. She turned her head, running her hand through her hair. "It's not a question of *liking*," she said, and added, "You do twist things around, don't you."

"Maybe *you* do," he muttered, and picking up a cushion, hurled it to the floor.

Her face cleared, and she said, as if relieved, "Yes, maybe I do."

After a moment he said, "So what's the scoop on this mother-son tandem?"

"No scoop. But they made an unlikely pair. You could see that a *pensione* wasn't their natural habitat. What a mom she was! Demanding, complaining — it was too hot, or too cold, the hills in Sienna were too steep, the buses were too crowded, the traffic too heavy, the churches too dark, the food too rich. I wonder he didn't throttle her with her Liberty silk scarf. But he was always polite and attentive, quick to close a shutter because the light hurt her eyes, or swat a fly whose buzzing annoyed her. She extolled his excellence as student, his virtues as a son, so devoted to her, etcetera, and he didn't protest, only looked a trifle uncomfortable. I tried to picture any of you in that plight. . . . "

"We've never been in it."

"I brag about you when you're not around. Don't you prefer that?"

"How can I prefer what I haven't experienced?"

"You are a stickler for accuracy, aren't you! You'd have liked Jerry's ma, she liked to be dead accurate about everything. Occasionally Jerry and I had a brief conversation, about something we'd both seen and particularly liked. But his mother resented being out of things, and the minute she reached for the conversational ball he gave it up."

"A paragon."

"No, but awfully nice. Her routine couldn't have been much fun for him. 'Dinner' at one o'clock every day — she couldn't stand the late Florentine hours — and pizza and brandy, of all things, at six o'clock in their room. With the shutters closed to keep out the sunset light and the bothersome sound of the bells. Also, she was certain that a bat was going to fly in. Only one evening did they go out, and with dire results."

"She got cholera."

"Almost as bad. She passed out in a trattoria and had to be carted off to hospital. Can you imagine, in an Italian ambulance. The hospital sounded medieval, thirty beds to a ward and the food served on tin plates. Not seeing them around, I assumed they'd left for Rome. Then at the end of the week I ran into Jerry and he told me the dismal tale.

He had a plastic bag of nightgowns and things he'd been washing out for her. What a rotten time for him! Sitting at her bedside all day and most of the night, and worrying about her — nobody seemed to know what was the matter with her, and she of course thought she was dying. Anyway, he was bringing her home that afternoon and he asked me to drop in and cheer her up."

"Which you gladly did." He blew across the top of his bottle.

"I didn't mind doing it. I said I'd stay while Jerry went out for a breather, but she said he didn't want to. He was lying on his bed — he'd been reading Robert Graves to her — and she was propped up against the pillows, wearing one of those fuzzy bathrobes that squeaked when she moved. On the headboard above her a lion was gnashing its jaws. She gave me a full account of the exciting event. Poor Jerry, he must have heard it a hundred times. Besides witnessing it."

"Perhaps among his many virtues was a taste for clinical details."

"Not this kind." She grimaced. "I couldn't figure him out. *Was* it devotion? Did he find her fascinating? Was he downtrodden? Or was he too a humdrum sort, temporarily disguised as an attractive young man?"

"I couldn't say."

She began to laugh. "I've got to tell you the details leading up to her 'attack' as she related them. 'I decided that Jerry should have one good evening meal before we left Florence, beefsteak, I thought, they say the beefsteak here is excellent. So at six-thirty we went out and walked around, we had to walk quite a while because there was nothing open that early. My legs were aching though I didn't tell Jerry that' (like fun she didn't tell Jerry that) 'because I didn't want to spoil his evening. Also, I'd had an intestinal disturbance all day, a very loose stool, but that seemed to be over. I hadn't had to move my bowels in maybe — what would you say, Jerry, about three hours?' Jerry nodded, and I pictured her getting up and moving her bowels from the top of the dresser to the desk, rather like a large bag of groceries."

He watched her, impassive.

She sipped at her drink. "Eventually, they found a trattoria that wasn't too big or too small or too empty or too crowded. . . ."

"Yes." His voice signified impatience.

"So they sat down, she — not surprisingly — facing the door, he the wall. 'We ordered a bottle of wine, a Valpolicella, because Jerry loves a good wine, as for me a bottle of wine can sit in my icebox for weeks, I don't care for drinking. Then I ordered the spaghetti alla bolognese, and Jerry ordered cannelloni. Or was it fettucine? Yes, I think it was the fettucine with butter and cream and Parmesan cheese, wasn't it, Jerry?' Just that once, he cracked a bit. He said, 'Mom, it doesn't really matter what I ate.' She said, 'No, but I like to get my facts straight. Then I ordered veal with mushrooms, *funghi*, they call them here, and Jerry, as was planned, had the beefsteak fiorentina, and I think it was zucchini, wasn't it, Jerry?' 'I don't remember,' Jerry said, and she said, 'Well, I do, it was the zucchini. We also ordered *insalata mista*, mixed green salad. Our first course came and I took a forkful and it was too salty. Jerry said his fettucine was good, though, and he poured some wine for me and I took a sip and all at once I began to feel funny, and I said to Jerry, Jerry, I'm beginning to feel funny. Wasn't that what I said?' 'Yes, I think it was,' Jerry said, but that didn't settle it. 'Well, it was either I'm beginning to feel funny, or I feel kind of funny, and that's the last thing I remember until I came to on the floor of that trattoria, saying I felt funny....'"

He was looking at her, uncomprehending, as if she had inadvertently lapsed into a language foreign to him.

Her voice gone flat, she said, "I thought you'd be amused. I was wrong. Sorry."

He shook his head, slowly. "I don't understand you," he said. "What's funny about a person passing out, wherever they are?"

"I didn't say *that* part was amusing." Her hand was clasped tight around the glass she was holding. "Let's skip it, shall we?"

As if she hadn't spoken, he went on, "You sat and listened to her, she probably thought you were her friend, that's why she spilled all that stuff, she thought you were interested in her. You do that to people, you *pretend*, so that later you can be 'amusing' about them." He spoke in a calm judgemental tone. "And then you make a big deal out of being 'polite' and 'kind'. The first commandment, Be polite and kind. I've heard it all my life."

"Julian, *please*. Let's not go into it. It was my mistake, an error in judgement, I apologize for it. You seemed interested, I was glad to have a chance to talk to you. It seldom happens, these days. But I shouldn't have gone on like that. It annoys you, I know."

He shrugged. "It's a free country."

The life had gone out of her face, the lightness out of her body. She sat there inert, her hands now lying like weights in her lap. Fine lines showed around her eyes and mouth. "You kept saying, Go on, and I tried, though it wasn't easy...."

"I tried, too! But pretty soon I got the message."

"What 'message'?" She lit a cigarette.

He got up and opened the glass doors. Cold air rushed in, and she shivered.

With his back to her, looking out into the dark, he said, musingly, "It's always the same message, isn't it? Your excellence, the deficiencies of others. Especially of ordinary people who don't pretend to be great—like your friends. You deliberately charm people, you seem to think it's rude not to turn it on, and then you do your hatchet job. You show them as contemptible, they like to eat hot-cakes and syrup, or they have the sniffles, or Italian lovers with flashing smiles." His soft voice glittered. "That woman who liked borders, you actually learned from her, you admitted it, but you had to put her down. She was cold and ungiving, no lady bountiful she, winning grateful smiles from beggars. She was a bad mother, she hadn't seen her kid in five years. Maybe the kid was better off without her, and she was smart enough to know it. But the woman travelling with her son was wrong too, wasn't she, she was a bore, and unattractive. Not like you. But her son loved her anyway." He swung around violently, his head thrust forward, spitting out his speech faster, faster. "It was a little morality, wasn't it, that's what it all led up to, you said to yourself, you said you had to get to the finish. You wanted to show me a good son and a dreary mother compared to a bad son and a . . . . " He stopped, letting his breath out furiously.

Not lifting her eyes, she said. "Why do you like to do that, Julian? Deliberately misinterpret. It's . . . ." She paused, went on. "It wasn't a 'morality', it never occurred to me to compare. . . ."

"But you did! In your mind you were always comparing, you even said it, Can you imagine *me* doing that. Point by point, you compared. *He* was clean and shining, I'm a mess. *He'd* just graduated, I'm a drop-out. *He* was agreeable, I'm surly. *He* washed his mother's nightgowns, I don't even put the kettle on. Did you really not hear what you were saying? Don't you ever listen to yourself? No, you don't, do you. If you did, you'd know it's all *shit*."

She struck her hands on her knees. "I've said I'm sorry." Her voice rose, thin edged. "Let's not talk about it. Let's not fight. It's very bad for you. Bad for both of us."

"Whenever I say what I think you call it fighting! What am I supposed to do, keep quiet all the time? Never have an opinion of my own? Sit and listen to you forever?"

She was looking at him as if she had never seen him before. Slowly, she said, "Sometimes I think you're . . . . "

"Crazy!" He pounced in. "Why don't you say it? You can't take it, can you, that one of your children isn't what you wanted him to be. You think it's a failure on your part, that's what you can't stand."

She jumped up, pressing her hands to her ears. "No, no! I was going to say, sometimes I think you're faking it, the whole thing, being sick, or unhappy — crazy, if you want to call it that — just to torture me!"

"What makes you think" — his tone was the more

insolent in being so calm — "that I'm all that concerned with *you?*"

She took a step towards him, eyes flashing with wrath, hands lifting. His hands, hanging at his sides, clenched. They faced each other for a blazing moment, then she cried, "Oh, go, please go! Go before I say something I'll regret!"

"But you can always say you're sorry, can't you. You've always been good at saying you're sorry." He went then, out of the room, down the hall, up the staircase, his light footsteps almost inaudible on the carpeted floors. A door closed. From somewhere else in the house came a whoop of young girls' laughter and, outside, children could be heard, talking and rustling through fallen leaves. There was the sound of rain falling.

She sat down carefully, her body rigid, as if she were in physical pain. She brought her hands flat down, fingers spread, on the table, and bending over said in a voice that seemed squeezed out of her. "I can't do it any more, I can't bear it, there *is* such a thing as hopeless...."

Children entered the house, calling her. She sat up abruptly, wiped at her eyes with the palm of her hand. When the two little boys came in she was kneeling on the hearth, crunching up newspaper. With her face averted, she said, "What about a fire to welcome your father? We need more wood, who's longing to bring in the wood?" She talked on in a bright artificial voice. When they had gone, she sagged again, sitting back on her heels, staring into the flames.

He appeared in the doorway. "May I use your car?" He spoke as if it affronted him, having to ask a favour.

"Yes, of course. The keys are in it." She poked at the fire. "You'll drive carefully, won't you. It's bound to be foggy."

"Yes," he said. "You needn't worry about your car."

She drew a breath. "You know it's not the car I worry about. Julian? I'm sorry I blew up."

He hunched his shoulders, frowning. "Yes. Well...I have to go."

She looked up at him. After a moment she said, "I *am* sorry. They're not just words. I love you. I make mistakes, and I regret them." In a steadier voice she went on, "We must all go on trying, mustn't we. I must try, and...."

The swift impatient intake of his breath seemed to strike her like a blow. She flinched, crouching there, and instead of finishing her sentence said, tonelessly, "Have a good time."

He hesitated, hunching deeper into his storm-coat. His face struggled, as if he too wanted to say something and could not, was physically unable to get the words out.

But she was not looking at him; she was gazing into the fire. When she did glance up, he had gone.

Inland beach

NORA AND MONICA, WITH NORA'S MOTHER AND MONICA'S children—Jean and Ben—and two friends of Jean's, arrived at the beach around midday. Another family party was leaving, laden with snorkels and swim-fins and a sleeping baby in a basket. The young father, stepping aside to make room for the new arrivals on the path down the dunes, said, "It's all yours," and gestured at the deserted cove beneath the dunes and the long white sandspit that ran out into the bay. Not even a boat in the bay, nothing but sky and sea and sand and, far off, the dunes across the water.

They had come to this inland beach to gather the shells for which it was noted and to have a change from surf swimming. Nora and Monica were delighted by the privacy and tranquility; the children were not.

"Dullsville," one of Jean's friends said, not quite *sotto voce*.

Ben read the sign beside the path. "*Danger. Strong Tides*." He looked disdainfully at the blue water, still as glass. "There aren't any waves. Not even a little old ripple."

Nora, for long a summer resident on Nantucket and an experienced sailor, said, "You can't judge the pull of the tide by the height of the waves, Ben. Away out there" — she pointed — "the bay empties through a narrow neck into the ocean. When the tide runs out, the suction is tremendous. You know what happens when you pull the plug out of the bathtub?"

Ben disregarded the simplification. "You'd get swept out to sea?"

"No, dummy. In a bathtub, you'd be swept down the drain," Jean said.

This reminded Ben of an incident in *Stuart Little*, and he told them about it over their picnic lunch. "So if I got swept out to sea," he finished, biting into a peach, "I'd just give three sharp tugs on my little string and you could haul me in again."

"Fat chance," Jean said, in the disparaging voice she was using these days with her nine-year-old brother, and helping themselves to fruit and cookies she and her friends skipped off on some private exploration.

Nora's mother and Ben constructed a drip-castle, with moats and towers and shell battlements. Nora and Monica lolled, lazily talking; the girls came back; they all went swimming.

The children, untiring, were still swimming when Nora and Monica settled down to shell gathering. The floor of the bay was like a mosaic, so richly encrusted was it with shells of all sorts coruscating under the limpid water.

Kneeling, the two women chose with care the special shells they wanted, their companionable silence broken by the shrieks and splashes of the children who were playing an underwater hide-and-seek game that they called Marco Polo.

Monica, one hand full of translucent orange shells, looked up and across the sandspit, where towels and blankets and beach-wraps made a bright hump on the sands. Ben was on the other side, all by himself, happily porpoising around. She waited for him to surface, then called to him. "Swim with the others, Ben! Come back on this side. Please." Turning to Nora, she said, "I know how bored he is with my saying that. And how bored I am saying it. Do you realize that for over twenty years I've been standing on beaches, bellowing, 'Stay with the other swimmers!'"

Nora — whose children, like Monica's older ones, were in college — said, "How lucky you are still to have someone to say it to." She was dabbling in the water with a graceful hand. In the other hand she held a mesh bag half full of shells. "I can't think what we're going to do with all these, can you? Shall we make sailor's valentines?"

"Or plaques saying *God Bless Our Home*, to surprise people with at Christmas. Your mother's putting hers in apothecary jars. She has about a hundred of them."

"So that's where they got to. I've been looking all over the house for those jars."

"I'm sure she could spare you a couple of dozen." Monica sat back on her heels, fondly looking at Nora's mother who with a book in hand was walking towards the dunes. The purple of her long full skirt, the pink of the silk shirt she had borrowed from Nora, the orange of her conical straw hat — these colours blazed against the scintillating sand. "If I could look like her when I'm eighty I wouldn't mind being old." She glanced across the sandspit, said, "Damn," and got up abruptly, leaving Nora immersed in her shell collecting. She ran across the spit, the sand burning her feet. I'm tired of bossing people around, she thought. I'll be glad when he's grown up.

To him she said shortly, "Ben, you're too old to forget rules. Come back with the others, and come at once." It vexed her to have to nag. He was just a few yards away, and only waist-deep, but rules were rules.

The water around him was indigo, though closer in it was colourless. Every pebble could be seen and schools of minnow darting zigzag. Miniature fern-fronds moved gently in their sunlit world. How beautiful it all was, the water and the light and the enameled sky. Perhaps as lovely a summer day as she would ever see. She watched Ben indulgently, not wanting to destroy her pleasure in the day with a battle of wills. After all, he wasn't doing anything, he wasn't ignoring her or disappearing from sight, as he had liked to do all week long in the tumultuous ocean surf. He was just paddling with his hands and doing a kind of on-the-spot marching.

"Come on, Benjamin," she said cajolingly. He said something in reply, and she frowned, reacting to his words without quite hearing them. "What? What did you say?"

"I said, I'm trying to come in, and I can't." He was smiling as if he were perplexed, but amused.

"Don't be silly," Monica said. "Of course you can come in."

"I can't. I can't get in."

Fear pricked at her heart, but only momentarily. He was so close to her — a few strides, and she could reach him. He was in no danger, and perhaps it was good for him to have some experience of the sea's strength. She waded into the water and said, "Now. Just swim, or walk, to me."

"I'm trying."

Hearing a note of alarm beneath the cheerfulness, she began to move towards him. She was still holding the shells in her hand, and waist-deep, thought, What shall I do with them? And answered herself, I'll hang on to them. Holding the shells made it clear that there was nothing seriously wrong. "Good, strong strokes," she said, wanting him to take care of this by himself.

He began swimming, his brown arms stretching well ahead of him, his feet kicking rhythmically. But he was not getting any closer to her. All at once, with a shudder of cold and surprise, Monica was up to her neck. The firm, sandy bottom had disappeared, and Ben was several yards from her. It's serious, she thought, it's a terrific current. She let the shells go and began to swim. With a few strokes, she was beside him. She put an encouraging hand on his back and, turning, saw that the shore was much farther away than it should have been. They were drifting fast.

"We'll take it easy," she told him confidently, while inwardly cursing her folly. All that talk about drains and currents and rules, and she had let this happen. Ben nodded, looking into her eyes with a trust and confidence that smote her heart. Together, they swam. Ben had to work much too hard. Why don't they teach the breaststroke nowadays? she wondered, and remembered her father teaching her, long before she had learned Ben's kind of fast, fancy crawl. It was fine for racing down a swimming pool, but it left him no staying power.

"Take it easy," she said, "It's not the Olympics."

The beach was deserted. No sign of the others. She began to realize the current was pulling them not only out, but down towards the end of the long spit of beach, beyond any reach of shore. This side of the bay was scalloped with coves, and with the tide running out from all of them —— "I'm tired," Ben said, and Monica grabbed his right arm, pulling him towards her. "Rest. Don't talk." Wavelets of dark water ran over them, around them. But it was warm water, the sun was warm, they could keep going for some time. "You be the cart," she said. "I'm the horse."

He did not smile. He sputtered along, his head thrown rigidly back. She dared not look towards shore, to measure their progress. She knew they should drift with the current, but if they did, could they make it back to shore? And what shore?

She stopped thinking. Ben was thrashing wildly. "You're — trying — to — drown — me! Let go!" Stupid, she thought, letting him go, of course he can't swim with one arm. At once he was upon her, his hands on her neck, clutching. She drew her feet up to her chest, made a heavy ball of herself, and went down, down. Lights sparked in front of her eyes. But he had released her.

Surfacing, she seized his arms, pushed him up so that his head was well out of the water. "Tread water," she ordered. "We're all right. Hear? We're getting back, but we have to be strong." She let him down again, still holding him by the arms, feeling by his lightness that he was obeying her. Her heart thundered as if it would burst out of her chest. His panic had scared her. And cost them dearly — the shore was farther away than ever. Behind Ben there was nothing but blue, endless, endless, until blue sky fell into blue water. But Ben was calm. His eyes, which had been full of terror, were brave and believing again.

"Ready?" she asked, and side by side they swam. If only she could tell him to float when he needed a rest! But there was no use; he was one of those people who couldn't float. Something to do with his centre of gravity or the way he breathed? She couldn't remember. She stole a look towards shore, and there, praise be, was Nora, up to her knees in water, her coronet of hair gleaming in the sun. How strong she looked, how reassuring, standing there firm as a rock.

"Don't — come!" Monica's voice rasped out, as if from the back of her head. Nora must stay there, out of the current, and *will* them back in.

"You're not far out," Nora shouted. "Can you touch bottom?"

Brilliant idea. Monica said to Ben, "You swim. I'll walk along beside you."

"OK." He was desperate with bravery.

But when she tried to stand, there was no bottom, and the current yanked her legs right out from under her. It was a nasty shock, after a moment of hope. But at least she knew what they had to do. They had to stay on the surface, swimming with the little waves that were running in to shore. No more treading water, no more reaching for the bottom.

Swimming along, very close to Ben, she tried to make plans. When he tires, she thought, I'll get him on his back, pull him along. But now, while they could, they must swim. She said — was it really her voice, so strained and gulping? — "I'll get behind and push your feet. Take four big strokes, and I'll push again."

It worked. The shore seemed closer. But Nora — Nora was ignoring them. She was kneeling in the sand, her back turned. She thinks we're all right, she's sorting her god-damn shells, Monica thought, and for a part of a second was bewildered, caught somewhere between incredulity and anger at such callousness. "Again," she said to Ben, and once more she said, and again, "Again." Her chest was burning. There was a fire where once her heart had been thundering.

Then Ben gave up. "Can't!" He gasped, swallowing salt water, choking. She grabbed him, tried to slam him on the back. "Tired . . . ahhhh" — on a long wail — "I'm drown-ing. We're going . . . out to sea." Panic-possessed, pitiful, he turned on her, arms flailing.

She held him off, thinking, I'll have to hit him. How? Her breath came hard from somewhere along her back-bone, as if her lungs, like her heart, had ceased to exist. She squeezed out, "You're all right. Ben!" But they were not all right. For the first time, Monica knew that she too was terrified.

"No! Oh — help me!" He flung back his head, eyes shut, face waxen, and as he struck out at her, sending up an iridescent spray, Monica saw his hand with the missing middle finger sheared off by the hoof of a horse that, rearing, had thrown him. The strong, broken little hand seemed to be saying something important about the nature of life, about its frailty and finitude.

Struggling with Ben, struggling for breath, her mind confused and strength spent, stricken with sorrow for her child whose choked laments, as they rocked together, crashed with sea sounds in her ears, Monica thought, It isn't worth it. She had used up her heart and lungs, steel bands were clamping around her shoulders and arms and her thighs. Why fight so bitterly, just to get back? And then, blessedly, peacefully, she knew that it would not be terrible to drown in the sun-struck blue.

At the same time, she was astonished to think that on this lovely summer's afternoon she was going to die. She thought, fleetingly, of her husband and her other children, of life and its bright joys, all vanished. But Ben — it must not be terrible for him. She must comfort him, teach him how to die. But first, quiet his shouting. It was unbearable.

It was not Ben shouting. It was Nora. Her voice came at them, ugly, strident, a rumble of harshness. "Cut out that crying...silly little fool...swim, stop bawling...swim."

The words, the sense of them, flayed Monica's spirit. How could she be so cruel to Ben, now? With an effort, she raised her head, wanting to protest, and through the water-splashed air saw Nora at the very end of the beach, swinging some kind of cumbersome rope. And she remembered, suddenly, that Nora's father and brother — the mother's husband and son — had been drowned in a sailing accident. What anguish this must be, for them!

So, with a great, death-defying resolution, she croaked at Ben, "Swim!" She shoved his feet and began it all again, shoving and swimming, shoving and swimming, her breath clattering out of her.

Then there was nothing to shove. Gone, she thought, indifferent. But she heard a great cry, and lifting her head from the tumble of water, she saw Ben sailing away from her, hanging on to a rope. Nora was laughing. Her white teeth shone.

Monica had a sensation of extreme joy: it was like some other moment of earthshaking happiness, she could not bother to remember where, or when. This was enough. Moments later, she was on the shore.

"Saved by a clothesline," Nora said exuberantly, and Monica dropped the dripping tangle of jerseys and shirts and fell into Nora's arms. She had not thought a woman's embrace would be so comforting, so strengthening. It flashed in her mind: We are the same, we are one. We know what birth and death are.

Nora was speaking to her. Monica tried to move but could not; she was heavy as stone. Jean was there too, and her friends behind her, silent and with shocked faces.

"Mother, Mother," cried Jean, "what's happened to you? Your face is all twisted!"

Nora said, "Darling, your mother has had a terribly hard swim. Let her rest."

Monica tried to put out an arm to Jean, but it fell limply down Nora's back.

"Are you all right?" Jean asked fearfully.

Monica nodded. "My face'll untwist soon." Her words sounded twisted too, as if she had been heavily drugged or had had a stroke, and she still had not the energy to move away from Nora who must be tired of holding her up, but kept saying, "Everything's all right. Ben's all right, you're all right." Her abundant golden hair had fallen from its coils and lay in wet strands over her shoulders, streaking Monica's face.

"How long were we out there?" Monica asked, stupidly, as if it mattered.

"About ten years."

"Am I laughing or crying?...Your mother. I suddenly remembered about — and I thought how awful if ——— "

"She didn't see a thing. She's down there in the cove, no doubt reading her study book on Zen. I just happened to look up, and at first I thought you and Ben were having a cozy little swim. And the girls didn't have an inkling. Just as well, I guess. One lost head and I'd have lost mine, gone plunging into the current after you or, more likely, have raced off to town to buy a life preserver. And you know how long it would have taken me to find a parking place." Nora's lightness was tonic, exactly what Monica needed. "Now the girls are finding out what happened. They're giving Ben the third degree."

Smiling, Monica was aware that her face felt less grotesque. Through the blanket Nora had wrapped around her she could feel Nora's hand massaging deep into her back, her shoulders. Warmth and well-being began to flood through her, and more than that, a great elation. So short a time ago she had thought with tranquility of death; now she was jubilant to be alive. How little it takes to satisfy us, she thought, life itself is enough. This chain of moments is what we have. The bad ones, of disappointment, failure, frustration, grief, terror. And the good ones, like this one, when all was splendid—sky and sea and grass-speared dunes, her daughter racing past, hair flying, brown legs shining.

"I'm taking Ben some cookies. He's ravenously hungry." Jean slowed down, stopped. "Are you all right, Mother? Your face is normal again."

Love, the greatest good, Monica thought, and waggled a hand at Jean. Love, friendship, physical strength. Drawing apart from her friend, she kissed her on the cheek. "Thank you, Nora."

"Oh, my dear...." Saying that, Nora's voice was unsteady. Recovering she said, "Ben, I thought you were a whole regiment of Arabs coming across the sand."

He was swathed in striped towels, trailing another that had been hitched around his waist. His eyes, caught in full sunlight, were like lapis lazuli.

A thread of memory unwound: Monica was one of a row of schoolgirls, teeth banded in wire, pigtails banded in elastic, messy tunics, ties askew, *Aeneids* dutifully open on their desks, listening with apathetic faces to the Latin mistress, shy, scholarly, English, describing to them the colour and texture of lapis lazuli. But Monica had not been bored. For that alone, for lapis lazuli, she had thought, the *Aeneid* is worth reading.

In Sienna, years later, she had wandered into an antique shop on San Pietro and had found a tiny bowl carved from the blue, gold-flecked stone and immediately had smelled the chalky smell of the schoolroom, seen the bushes weighted with purple lilac outside the window, heard the precise light voice of the teacher and, from a distance, the *kthwop* of tennis ball on backboard.

Now, seeing the colour, gold-dusted by the sun, in her young son's eyes, she was startled with pleasure and put out her hand to gently touch his face. His fair hair had dried in stiff wisps around his ears; beneath the skin's summer brown there was a touch of pallor.

He looked at her, taking her hand, twisting with his fingers the rings she wore on hers, and said gravely, "I'm sorry, Mother."

"Sorry!" She was incredulous, because for her there was only rejoicing. Bending to hug him she felt sudden hot tears on her cold cheeks, salt mingling with salt, pain with joy, and was swept back to that other moment when, tears of happiness spilling from her eyes and running over her sweaty face and into her damp and tangled hair, she had first looked at this child, scarlet and wrinkled, angrily mewing, still tied to her by the primal lifeline. What purity of bliss that had been. The rocking, explosive moment of birth, then all at once a liquid soft rippling — she herself a sand carving slipping heavily, languorously through deep sunlit waters. For an instant, piercing in its sweetness, she relived that moment when the universe had stood still, suspended in joy that had at its centre her newborn son and herself.

"Mother?" Worried by the tears that prickled his face, brushing them off, he drew away to look at her.

And she was recalled to this moment, and to her duty. She could not burden him with gratitude for the joy his birth had given her. She whispered, "We're a fine team, you and I," and released him.

With the unstudied courtliness that was part of his affectionate nature, he dropped a quick kiss on her hand and was off, careering across the hard sand, tossing away the towels as he ran, with arms outstretched like the wings of the white gull that, above him, slowly stroked on the wind blowing off the sea.

Prairie spring

WHEN MY MOTHER TOLD ME THAT MR. AND MRS. BEARDSLEY were expecting a daughter, I was surprised but not incredulous. From the Bible I knew that elderly women did occasionally bring forth sons, usually after due warning from an angel. I assumed that Mrs. Beardsley had been assigned a daughter, though she had probably not learned about it from an angel. It was more likely that Mr. Beardsley had told her that he expected her to have a daughter, and that she had answered, "Very well, John, if that is what you wish."

The Beardsleys' green-shingled bungalow, half hidden behind a high caragana hedge, was not far from our house — St. Peter's Rectory — in the small Saskatchewan town where I lived as a child. Elms and Manitoba maples lined the dirt road that ran in front of our house, and shaded the echoing wooden sidewalk that led from the main street, past the rectory and church, and on due west a short distance beyond the Beardsleys' house. There, by a clump of wild-rose bushes, the sidewalk came to a halt, and stepping off it one stepped onto the prairies. The trees had already straggled to a stop, as though they had long since found futile any attempt to invade that vast space.

In June, the Beardsleys' hedge was rich with honey-sweet yellow blossoms, and later with shining crisp pods which, when split open, made fine whistles. Protected by the greenery, my older brother and I supposed that Mr. Beardsley could not identify us as the rector's children, and blew raucously on pods plucked from his property, to vex him as he sat in his deck chair in his secluded garden. He never so much as glanced up from his reading. But the impressive thing about this neighbour of ours was that he was able to express an all-embracing hostility without having to articulate it. In his presence I felt both guilty and stupid, for he gave me the impression that he knew the depth of my wickedness but could not find it interesting. His eyes, bitter blue and slightly prominent, seemed unable to find an object worthy of their inspection. They were usually trained on the empty air, and if by chance I moved across their gaze I felt myself belittled.

Mrs. Beardsley was very good to my brother and me, giving us attractive presents for our birthdays and at Christmas, and always having at hand a treat to please us — a bar of butterscotch in a plaid-patterned box, a bottle of raspberry drops, or a tin of humbugs. Sometimes, having heard our voices, she would come to the garden gate and invite us to come in for lemonade which she poured from a tall cut-glass pitcher into squat cut-glass tumblers. With monogrammed tea-napkins on our laps, we sat swinging our feet, devouring thin slices of bread and butter and thick slices of plum cake, and replying, when our mouths were not too full, to her inquiries about our parents, our baby brother, our schoolwork. (We did not inquire about Mr. Beardsley, who was never present at these times.) Silver voiced, silver haired, Mrs. Beardsley was a small sweet-faced woman with a delicate air of serenity. Nothing about her, save the colour of her costume, seemed to change. Her hats were always folded velvet toques, like those in newspaper pictures of Queen Mary, ornamented with a glistening spun-glass feather. In the folds of her fichu hung a small gold locket, and in her belt was tucked a lacy white handkerchief scented with cologne 4711.

Mr. Beardsley was to be seen with absolute regularity at church and on his daily noontime promenade which coincided with our dash home from school for lunch. He carried a gold-topped cane, sending up a smart tap-tap from the grey boards of the sidewalk. His stride was long, and Mrs. Beardsley — much shorter than he — had to sacrifice her dignity by trotting to his walk. He perhaps considered her kind greeting all the attention we deserved, and ignored us, unless my father was in view, preparing to set out in his Ford touring car for two or three days of parochial visiting. Then, directing his steps and thus his wife's in our direction, he would doff his hat and say, "Good morning, Rector! Off on your rounds, I see. Well, *bon voyage!*"

Our parish, which contained the town and a scattering of hamlets and isolated farmhouses, was in an area of southern Saskatchewan that had been settled towards the end of the nineteenth century. These early colonists were mostly English or Anglo-Irish gentry who, bringing with them their servants and their household possessions, had come as Empire builders to the prairies, to see a new fortune in the new world. None had succeeded in this ambition, but though their incomes had dwindled away their spirit had not. Now with their children grown and dispersed about the continent — some reversing their parents' direction had returned to the "old country" — these high-hearted pioneers were enjoying a vigorous old age, occupying themselves in civic and church affairs, and pursuing their hobbies: bee-keeping, photography, playing chess by mail, and golf on a stubbled course pitted with gopher holes down which many costly golf balls disappeared.

There were a few remittance men and some other Britishers of family and education who had sought adventure or independence in the colonies. These were usually bachelors who seemed to enjoy, each in his own fashion, the freedom of this prairie community with its sporting and genteel traditions, and its opportunities to be indolent or energetic, sociable or withdrawn, at whim.

And there were the Beardsleys. They had arrived in Saskatchewan before the outbreak of the World War, as it was known in those days. Why they had left England or what they had left behind no one knew. This was not in itself unusual. There were on the prairies other immigrants whose manners and speech furnished an easily identifiable background but who kept their own counsel as to why they had forsaken it. Respect for another's reticence about his past was not only in the British tradition of reserve but a cardinal point in the etiquette of any pioneer settlement.

The Beardsleys were subtly different though, in that

their reticence extended, very courteously, into the present and still managed never to be questionable, never to hint at anything so vulgar as a mystery. In appearance they were the epitome of the respectable, the well-bred "retired", the right thinking. They seldom expressed opinions but behaved at all times like people with the correct ones. Mr. Beardsley, with his wife at his side, always entered the church door precisely five minutes before the service was to begin, was a member of the Vestry, gave an appropriate subscription each year to the fund for Empire and Dominion Day celebrations and on these occasions decorated his house patriotically with red, white, and blue bunting. He applauded politely at performances of Gilbert and Sullivan given by the local Savoyards. He read the London *Times* — a fortnight or more late — and subscribed to *Punch* and the *London Illustrated News*, which lay with their mailing creases beautifully flattened out on a polished table in the Beardsleys' sitting room, which managed to be crowded but never untidy. The regularity of his habits, the impeccability of his dress, his healthy colouring all gave evidence of a life well ordered and composedly shared by his wife.

How remarkable then that these people, so settled in their ways, were to have a child. A daughter who, according to my next snippet of information, had just set sail from England. I abandoned the notion of an infant. It must be an orphan they were adopting, possibly from a Dr. Barnardo Home. This thought gave me a very bad feeling of which I could speak to no one because it was too terrible. In those days conversation in front of children was carefully censored, and I was not supposed to know, but did know, the nightmarish story of the Barnardo child who had been imported by the local butcher to be an apprentice in his shop. Forced to sleep in an unheated shed, the boy had frozen to death one ferocious winter's night. What if the Beardsleys' orphan met a similar fate?

Then one bright September morning as I was coming home to lunch I saw Mr. Beardsley approaching down the dusty road, accompanied by Mrs. Beardsley and another lady, as tall as Mr. Beardsley and dressed all in brown. Mrs. Beardsley called out to me, and I stopped.

Thus I met the daughter the Beardsleys had been expecting, a middle-aged lady called Miss Beardsley, who had to be curtsied to, and who for an intimidating moment looked too much like her father for comfort. She had the same Roman nose, the same way of holding her head so that it jutted forward slightly. But immediately I felt that the effect was not menacing in her, as it was in her father, but showed an anxiety to please, as if she were bending her head with every effort to be agreeable. The brown gloved hand that took mine was timid. She was shy — the first adult I had ever recognized as shy. She glanced away from me, and back again, and said "Well!" in a kind of bright and trembling voice. "So you are the rector's little girl, how nice." And she dabbed at the tendrils of brown hair escaping from under her brown velours hat.

My mother was amused when I expressed surprise, and some disappointment, about Miss Beardsley. Apparently she had known that the daughter the Beardsleys were expecting would be a grown woman, not an infant or an orphan for Mr. Beardsley to mistreat. From all that was left unsaid by my mother and her friends I sensed that the arrival of Miss Beardsley, like the expected arrival of a baby, was something not to be talked about. When my mother had told me that *she* was expecting a baby she had said that I must keep it a secret, and had neglected to tell me after he was born that it was no longer a secret. For several weeks I refused to speak of him except at home, or to publicly acknowledge in any way the existence of this baby whom privately I crooned over and attempted to beguile with songs and rattles and rocking. But the reticence about Miss Beardsley's appearance on the scene had not the quality of a delightful secret shared, and I was aware that it had something to do with the way people felt about Mr. Beardsley.

I was particularly aware of it one afternoon when my mother gave a tea for Miss Beardsley. I had been told either to go off and play or to make myself useful in passing sandwiches and cakes. Curious, I chose to do the latter, and as I was proffering shortbread someone asked Miss Beardsley a casual question about her life in England. She put her teacup down, as if to give her entire attention to her answer. "I'm afraid I got about very little," she said. "You see, my aunt, who brought me up, was never very well, so we led a lazy, quiet life together. I'm afraid I'm a rather useless sort of person."

The other ladies pooh-poohed such a notion, which caused her to blush, as if embarrassed at having called attention to herself. "When my aunt died last spring," she went on, "there was really nothing I could do and no further reason for me to stay in England." She glanced with mild anxiety at her mother.

Mrs. Beardsley spoke up. "We came away from England," she said, "directly after Constance was born. My husband did not think it would be suitable to bring a young child to such an uncertain life."

Her listeners, some of whom had themselves brought young children to this same "uncertain life", received the explanation in silence. It was as if they had a tacit agreement to say nothing, knowing that no polite comment could be made that would not somehow have implicitly condemned Mr. Beardsley's cruel and unusual treatment of his wife and child.

The subject was changed. Mrs. Beardsley and her daughter took their leave early, no doubt to attend to their lord and master. The other ladies, stuffing embroidery into tapestry bags, permitted themselves to speculate on the puzzle of Miss Beardsley's sudden and belated appearance in her parents' lives. Had she asked, on the death of the invalid aunt, if she might come to Canada? Had Mrs. Beardsley urged that she be invited? Or had Mr. Beardsley, noting that his frail wife was aging, decided that his daughter would be of use to him, a suitable housekeeper when his wife should die?

My mother, evidently feeling called upon to offer some charitable explanation, suggested that Mr. Beardsley had realized that it was his duty to provide a home for his daughter, but this notion was roundly rejected.

"At any rate," someone said, "having her daughter here is doing Hannah Beardsley a world of good."

I too had noticed a change in Mrs. Beardsley. There was an almost sprightly air about her, and she smiled not just out of kindness but out of happiness too. She and her daughter could be heard chatting away, their fluting voices birdlike, as they took their required morning exercise.

Mr. Beardsley, by contrast, seemed more silent than ever, and there was something vengeful about the way he swung his cane and brought it down with a sharp smack into the dust. Now that there were three of them, they had to walk on the road, as the sidewalk was too narrow. It seemed to be the chief difference his daughter's presence made to him, that where once he had had one woman beside him he now had two. Two women to promenade with him, to toast his muffins and brew his tea, two women to sit with him in church. Two voices, instead of one, to join with his in prayer. At Divine Worship, as nowhere else, Mr. Beardsley enjoyed the sound of his own voice, and it was particularly fine to hear him recite the General Confession, declaring himself a miserable offender with no health in him. Above him, in stained glass, St. George slew a vicious green dragon with a hooded neck.

In October we had our first snow, followed by a brief and beautiful Indian summer. Miss Beardsley, who had brought out a fur neckpiece, put it away, and intoxicated perhaps by the golden air and flawless, huge sky, went about hatless. Once we saw her sturdily tramping across the rutted prairie. It was late afternoon, and the harvest sun hung, a great red ball, in the western sky. Seeing the solitary figure against the fiery sun made me realize that I had never seen Mrs. Beardsley go anywhere unaccompanied. Previously, her husband had been her constant escort; now she went out to tea occasionally with her daughter, or arm in arm, neatly stepping, deep in conversation, they went off to do their marketing. One morning when I had been kept home from school with a cold, they dropped in with a present for me, a bag of oranges — a luxury in a prairie rectory. They loosed their wraps and consented to sit down for a moment, seeming pleased with themselves but a little nervous, as if they were on an escapade. When the allotted moment was up they hurried away, explaining that Mr. Beardsley had a touch of lumbago, and had had to stay home. Miss Beardsley had promised to play chess with him before lunch. Picturing Mr. Beardsley seated at the game table, waiting, I understood their haste.

When the weather became cold Miss Beardsley looked miserable. Her long nose turned red, and suspended from the end of it was always a glistening drop of which she was unaware. Her eyes watered, and she clutched her fur around her neck, the flat beady-eyed fox head snapping at her ear. When she came to the parish hall to conduct the weekly meetings of the Little Helpers — an organization whose leadership she had eagerly assumed — she gathered us around the pot stove for our hymn singing and prayers, and kept her hat and coat on while from the tinny piano she directed us in games of Musical Chairs, "London Bridge", "The Farmer's in the Dell", and "Here Go the Blackbirds". She gave us boxes shaped like pyramids for our Advent offerings. I stuffed mine with counterfeit money made from the heavy silver-foil wrappings on packages of tea. Miss Beardsley congratulated me on the weight of my offerings, and when I saw her go out into the cold twilight, carrying the boxes in her needlepoint bag, I was stabbed with remorse. Not because of the Eskimo children who in their mission school were awaiting my pennies, but because Miss Beardsley would be so disappointed, opening my pyramid and finding in it fake nickels. She would think it another trick on herself. I wanted to apologize to her, but instead I took the cowardly way out and asked God to forgive me. Miss Beardsley made no mention of it either. She was too timid to reprimand me, and did not have it in her to make a joke of my prank.

We had our first blizzard early in the new year. Mr. Beardsley, whose lumbago had returned and kept him house-bound through the holidays, must have sprung from his bed of pain, fully recovered, at the shrill arctic blast. For on the next day, when the wind had ceased to blow and the temperature had dropped to thirty below, he chose to resume his preprandial walk. Our teacher, dismissing us for the noon recess, had ordered us to hurry straight home, not to stop and play in the wind-sculpted, dazzling white drifts for fear of being frostbitten. Suddenly, Mr. Beardsley loomed up ahead of us, making his way through this world of ice and snow, accompanied by his ladies. In their long Hudson seal coats and matching fur hats and muffs, their breath frosting the fur around their faces, they looked like two visitors from a zoo as they trod cautiously in the slippery tracks left by cutters and sleighs. Mr. Beardsley's tall astrakhan hat was pulled down over his ears, his moustache was rimed, but he marched along almost jauntily, his black boots squealing against the hard snow, his cane tapping sharply. He seemed to enjoy that walk in the merciless cold. Perhaps he was warmed by the exercise of his authority over the two women.

It was not long before certain facts came to light, unveiled by his wife. Never in a spirit of criticism — it is possible that like countless women of her generation and kind she believed that her duty was to bend her will to that of her husband. Anyway, it would not have been seemly to speak of private griefs or resentments. But when the one extraordinary fact about herself became known — that she was not childless but the mother of a fifty-two-year-old daughter — it seemed natural to mention other circumstances which had not previously been known, none of which actually contradicted anything she had said before.

She had been married at seventeen, and had been eighteen when Constance was born. Mr. Beardsley had been in poor health and had found the baby "very trying to his nerves". When the baby was six weeks old it had been necessary for his health to spend some time in a warmer climate. They had left Constance with her nanny and gone on a "little trip" to Italy. The little trip had lengthened into fifteen years and had led them eventually to the bungalow on the Canadian prairies. They had never returned to England and their child. Mr. Beardsley spent those Continental years, I suppose, teaching his young wife the hard lesson she had to learn, that it was he, and only he, who was to occupy her attention. He had said that he very much wanted Constance to have an English upbringing. Later he had felt that Constance should stay with his sister, who had brought her up, and take care of her in her declining years. Because she had missed her daughter so much, Mrs. Beardsley was reported to have said, she had found it easier not to speak of her.

I knew that was a lie: Mr. Beardsley had told his wife not to speak of their daughter. But it would have been unthinkable for such a woman, bound equally by her marriage vows and her regard for propriety, to stoop to the humiliation and embarrassment of exposing her husband as a man too difficult to live with. And if she knew the secrets of his hard, cold heart, she never revealed them. Mr. Beardsley was a man for whom it was not sufficient simply to feel his alienation from other men but who was driven to find a particularly forbidding stage on which to display his otherness. The very look of the landscape he had chosen, the hard sweeping loneliness of it, must have added to his feeling of injured isolation. He could not have lived alone, unattended, nor could he have tolerated the presence of a stranger who might peep and pry, who would not be instantly sensitive, as his wife was, to what he was thinking or feeling.

When his sister had died, he had sent for his daughter. The expression "sent for" was connected in my mind with the T. Eaton mail-order catalogue, and I visualized Mr. Beardsley filling out the required form, mailing it off, and then awaiting delivery of the goods — in this case a younger more vigorous model of his wife, who would take care of him when his wife was no longer able to do so, would flatten the creases in his magazines, would dust his chessmen and his collection of snuff boxes, and serve his meals.

But Mr. Beardsley, however practical he had been in his reckoning, had failed to take into account the unpredictable ways of the human heart. How could he have known that his obedient wife had for all these years been storing up her love for the child she had borne fifty-two years earlier? Or that, unaccustomed to love, his daughter would so easily respond to it? How chagrined he must have been to find affection and happiness flourishing beneath his roof, to see his wife and daughter mildly blooming, rejoicing in each other's company. Dutiful as the two women were, quick to respond to his commands and demands, they were, indubitably, happy. The sight of them, not victims but gentle victors, must have been more than he could bear. Foiled, for once, it was he who died.

His death was abrupt and public, not at all the kind of thing he would have cared for. I learned of it on Maundy Thursday morning. My mother was preparing breakfast, and in a matter-of-fact though subdued voice she told me what had happened. It gave me quite a thrill of mixed excitement and horror to picture the scene — my father's concern as Mr. Beardsley toppled over, the dismay of the congregation, the solemn yet distasteful commotion that death, I supposed, must always make.

As was his custom, Mr. Beardsley had been attending the Wednesday evening Lenten service. Following the collects for the day, the Litany had been read, and it was during that reading that Mr. Beardsley collapsed. The Litany, as I was aware, contains a special plea for deliverance from sudden death. Perhaps just an instant after saying, "Good Lord, deliver us," Mr. Beardsley had been struck down. I knew the episode would immensely appeal to my brother, and was about to dash off to tell him, but my mother called me back. I was to take tea up to Mrs. Beardsley and Miss Beardsley who had, it seemed, spent the night in our spare room.

I would have preferred to know that Mr. Beardsley had spent the night there, cold and dead, with the eiderdown pulled up to his chin. At least death would have imposed on him a silence even more reliable than his habitual silence in life. But bereaved people wept and sobbed, and grief was alarming to behold. Once when my father had taken me on his parochial rounds we had gone to a farmhouse to visit a woman whose husband had died. I had not known until then that adults could cry, and it was not a sight I wanted to witness again.

Because my mother disregarded my feeble protests, I was forced to tell her that I could not take the tea up because I did not want to see Mrs. Beardsley and Miss Beardsley crying. "They won't be crying," she said, and added, "they aren't people of that sort. Go along up now, before the tea gets cold."

Outside their door I put the tray down on a bookcase and tapped softly, hoping they would not hear me. But Mrs. Beardsley's voice bade me enter, and Miss Beardsley opened the door and smiled down at me. She looked rested and serene. Her hair — here and there touched with grey — was unpinned and fell about her shoulders. She was wearing my mother's Japanese kimono with flowers embroidered on the back of it. Mrs. Beardsley, still in the big brass bed, sat up against the pillows, drawing her knitted bedshawl about her with a little exclamation of pleasure. "Good morning, my dear," she said. And "Tea! How lovely!"

"Now, where shall we put the tray?" Miss Beardsley wondered, and glanced about the room as if there were any number of places to put it, and all the time in the world to decide.

"Perhaps on the table by the window?" suggested her mother. It was the only table in the room, but she made it sound like an interesting suggestion and one that she had enjoyed making.

Miss Beardsley took one end of the tray and together, awkwardly, we set it down. "There!" She seemed pleased by our accomplishment, and reaching over the table, pulled up the window shade and pushed aside the lace curtains. Looking out, she said in a kind of marvelling voice, "Why I do believe spring is coming."

I saw it too, that subtle change in the way the world looks that heralds the start of a new season. The sun had a golden shimmer, there in the pale sky, giving promise of warmth to come. Even from inside the house I could almost feel the first spring thaw in the air. Soon the air would smell again of earth. The thick icicles twisting down from the eaves were already cloudy around the edges, and the snow that had been hard-packed against the fence looked moist, fine for building igloos and snowmen which would gradually crumble and melt away until one day there would be nothing left of them but the pieces of coal we had used for the eyes, lying in a great splotch of muddy snow on the bare earth.

"Spring is very beautiful on the prairies," Mrs. Beardsley remarked. "It is always a joy."

"Yes, I expect it is." Miss Beardsley spoke in a gentle confident way, pouring tea for her mother. Turning away from the window, I saw how the morning sun lit up the gay red of Miss Beardsley's kimono as she carried the tea across the room to her mother.

Two women

THESE TWO WOMEN, ARIADNE AND ANDREA, HAD MET A year and a half earlier on Parents Day at the school their daughters attended. They had talked over mid-morning coffee and had sat together during a performance of the *Mikado* in the course of which Ariadne had mopped her eyes.

"Little kids singing. It always gets to me," she had said.

Andrea had been surprised. In their two-hour acquaintance she had thought Ariadne very self-possessed, slightly hard edged, certainly not a person easily moved to tears.

A week later, Ariadne had called to invite Andrea to lunch. But Andrea almost never bothered with lunch. It ruined the afternoon. Mornings were mornings, afternoons were for teaching or practising, and she often had late afternoon rehearsals. She played viola in a Long Island orchestra, and occasionally in a small chamber orchestra.

"Any old time then," Ariadne had said. "We could have a cup of tea. Or a cup of gin if you'd prefer."

They made a date for Andrea's first free afternoon.

They went down to Soho, where a friend of Andrea's was having a show. After that they took to meeting quite frequently, going to museums or galleries, sometimes to a film, sometimes taking their children on a jaunt.

Andrea was a native of Melbourne, and had lived there until she was twelve years old.

"You don't talk like a Strine," Ariadne told her. "And you don't look like a Strine."

"How do Strines look?"

"The best-looking ones are marsupials."

Andrea laughed. "A thousand thanks!"

"Let's take the kids up to the zoo some day and look at the duck-billed platypus. I love those l'il things. Come to think of it, you're sort of like a platypus."

"My webbed feet? My habit of laying eggs?"

"You're sensitive, and you're very rare. Also it's obvious that you're a mammal."

Andrea pulled a face. She would have liked to have small breasts, like Ariadne.

The two friends talked about women's lives and E.R.A., about urban politics and problems, about places they had been and books they liked, about children — in particular their own — and occasionally about their husbands. Sometimes they argued. Ariadne was excited by every technological advance no matter what its threat to the human race. Andrea had fired off many letters protesting the Concorde; she circulated petitions against nuclear fission power-plants and wrote regularly to her congressman about endangered species. Unlike Ariadne she was not interested in space travel, and science fiction bored her.

She liked to play Schoenberg and Berg, and George Rochberg and George Crumb, composers whose works, Ariadne said, made her "long for Tchaikovsky with all the stops pulled out." And Ariadne was mad for animals, whether or not endangered. On the Westchester County farm that had been in her husband's family for three generations they kept thoroughbreds, Charolais cattle and black-eyed sheep. She was thinking of buying some buffaloes. She had three Border collies, and four cats, not counting the ones that lived in the barns.

Andrea had a cat, a Siamese, but she showed a preference for people rather than animals, and, specifically, for musicians, writers and painters. Her husband, Teddy, whom she had married at nineteen, was a composer, and taught theory and composition at Columbia. They had a small house in the country, not far from the farm where Ariadne spent weekends and part of the summer, and a cooperative apartment on West End Avenue which they rented for July and August to summer-school faculty.

Andrea's parents lived in Seattle. Her father was a retired engineer, her mother taught piano. Ariadne had a very rich Greek father and an alcoholic mother who lived "at the bottom of some Alp or other." When she was going to Kenya with her father, on a safari, Andrea said to her, "You're only going to look at animals, aren't you? You're not going to shoot them?"

"Are you bonkers? Shooting's against my principles. The only living thing I'd consider shooting is a mortally wounded animal. Or my mother — except that she doesn't deserve the attention."

Ariadne conveyed the impression that she had a lively and gratifying sexual life with Oliver, and always made a great adoring fuss over him, and over Teddy on those occasions when they met. Andrea thought Oliver rather stuffy, but supposed he could not help it. His course of life had been prescribed at birth: St. Bernard's, Groton, Yale, Yale Law School. He bought his clothes at Tripler & Co., read *Screw* and *Playboy* and spy stories, and fell asleep at concerts. An ancestor of his, whose portrait hung in the dining room of their East Side brownstone, had signed the Declaration of Independence. Oliver referred to him as The Signer. The first time he had done so, Andrea had laughed, supposing that he was being flippant.

Andrea was reticent about her sexual life with Teddy; she was by nature reticent about that most intimate aspect of her life. Recently, in response to a direct question of Adriadne's — casually enough put — she had admitted that she had had "affairs". Of which, she truthfully added, she had not before spoken to anyone. Ariadne's agitated reaction had taken her aback.

"How could you do that? You made a marriage vow, how could you break it?" She lit a cigarette from the one she was already smoking, stubbed it out. "I could never do that. I make a promise, I keep it. Oh, there are men that turn me on, I don't deny that, but it's the red light, where I'm concerned."

"Do you know, I've always assumed you'd had lovers? You're easy about sex, frank about enjoying it, and you like men so much."

"Who're these men I like so much?"

"Well — Oliver, for instance."

"He's my husband, for God's sake! I promised to like him, didn't I, even if he is a bastard? They're all bastards." She laughed, glancing sidewise at Andrea who laughed, too, while disagreeing. "Not *all* of them."

Ariadne had that knack of never seeming busy, though in fact she was. Her father would blow into New York, demanding attention; her in-laws lived there. To her two daughters she was a spirited and devoted mother; she was dutiful about Oliver's career — going to required dinner parties and receptions and benefits; two mornings a week she worked with "disadvantaged" pre-school children. She had two houses to run. But whenever Andrea called to propose a meeting, Ariadne's response was unhesitating. "Of course I'm not busy, I just have to give tea to Oliver's ancient aunts. One's deaf and the other's blind. Or maybe it's the other way round, I forget. Anyway, it won't take all afternoon." Or, "What would I be doing? Bring the kids round for a swim. I'll come get you. No, it's no trouble, I'd like to do that. Besides, dryads shouldn't drive cars."

Which amused Andrea, who, accompanied by her viola, regularly drove through fair weather and foul at all hours of the day and night.

Ariadne and her children spent July at her father's ranch in Wyoming. She wrote almost every day — wonderful letters about children and animals and fish and flowers and birds and weather, very amusing, often illustrated by clever little cartoons. And always very affectionate, as were Andrea's infrequent letters to her.

On the first of August, she called. "I just this minute rolled in. I had to call you, straight off."

"You sound out of breath. Are you on your way to a fire?"

"I'm being consumed by flames." Her voice had in it the slight *vibrato* that Andrea had heard several times in recent months, and that always gave her an obscurely uneasy sensation.

Andrea said, "Come over. I'll help quench the flames." And after a moment, "Are you there?"

"In a manner of speaking. Can I come right now?"

"I'd love it. Bring the children. Mine are still at camp, but. . . ."

"Mine're down at the stables, I'll never be able to pry them loose. Oh, Gilda foaled last night. Wouldn't you know I'd miss that, dammit?"

"Nothing went wrong, did it?"

"No, nothing went wrong. I'm just so fond of Gilda. I wanted to be with her in her first travail."

Ariadne accepted Andrea's hug with unusual restraint. Her back was rigid. Andrea could feel the tension in the muscles.

"You need an Alexander treatment," she said, off-handedly. "See what your plants have done, the ones you brought me in May? I've got a perennial border at last, thanks to you. Isn't the phlox lovely, all in bloom?"

"Anything would bloom for you."

"No, those were very high-class plants. Would you like a drink?"

"I've brought one. One bottle's for your cellar. The chilled one's for now." She had carried it over in a silver champagne cooler, which she stood on the ground between their chairs. "Tell me all about your summer. What a pen-pal you turned out to be. Four measly letters plus a postcard view of Puget Sound.... Let it ring, why don't you, it's probably some chump wanting to know if you're watching television."

"It was unimportant," Andrea reported, a minute later. "But I have to answer, it might be Teddy. He said he'd call today. Did I tell you he's in Britain for a month? At the moment in an awful wax because the clarinettist he wrote the Festival piece for has inconveniently broken his arm. Darn, there it goes again."

Returning, she went on, "Or it might be the camp, to say Joan's been bitten by an asp or Tony's fallen off a mountain peak."

"Have some more champers."

"I still have some."

"Have some more." Ariadne poured the wine recklessly. It bubbled over the rim of the glass. "Doesn't matter, there's more where that came from. Oh, God!" She clapped her hands over her ears. "I'll tear that thing out by the roots!"

Smiling, Andrea came back. "It was that bossy tympanist calling about the party he's determined to have — the orchestra's celebrating its fiftieth birthday — he asked me if I wanted to bring a hot dish for sixteen people or a hot dish for eight. Guess which one I chose."

"I love you." Ariadne's voice was low. Her head was

bent, and her hair, glossed by the sun, was blue-black, the centre parting very straight and white.

"Because I'd rather cook for eight than sixteen?"

Ariadne repeated in the same low, shaking voice, "I love you, Andrea. I love you. Do you understand?"

Andrea sat down. She reached out and took Ariadne's rigid hand in her own. "Oh, Ariadne, I'm so *sorry*. I had no idea. . . . I'm so sorry. What are we going to do?"

"Nothing. Don't worry about it, it's not your problem. I had to tell you, that's all. For every letter I sent you, I tore up two. I knew it was cowardly to write it, I had to say it, face to face."

"You were right to tell me, I'm glad you did. And that you didn't put it in a letter, because I'd have —— " She stopped, deeply affected by Ariadne's words, honoured by them, but confused, shaken. For her to have so exposed herself! That took courage. To comfort, she stroked Ariadne's bare brown arm, making soothing sounds, as if her friend had a bruise that could be stroked away.

"I'm sorry." Ariadne got up, abruptly. "I can't take it, I'd better go. Don't come to the car with me. I'll call you. Some day. I know you'll answer that bloody telephone, it might be your husband or your kids calling." Her attempt at a smile sat askew on her anguished face.

Andrea reproached herself for not having paid attention to the signs. For the signs, she now saw, had been there all along. In the compliments, the gifts, the attentions, in Ariadne's willingness to drop everything in order to be with her, in innumerable favours small and large, in the rather mannish style of dressing she had over the last months adopted. With all these Ariadne had been courting her. She had refused to notice. All she had noticed was the *vibrato* in Ariadne's telephone voice. But what sort of wildly egotistical person would she be if she assumed that everyone whose voice trembled was in love with her?

Thoughts of Ariadne preoccupied her. She wanted very much to see Ariadne, she found painful the prospect of losing a dear and valued friend whose company she enormously enjoyed, and with whom she felt on such intimate, easy terms. But she could not call Ariadne; she would not have called a man whose love she could not reciprocate. What would she say? I would love to see you but let's just be ordinary friends? She would wait for the sexual passion to pass. People fell in love, but they fell out of love when there was nothing for passion to feed on.

Then Ariadne called her. "I couldn't hold out any longer."

"Why should you? I've missed you. Come and have tea."

"It's only three o'clock. I'd ruin your afternoon."

"I'd love to see you. Please come." She spoke as fondly as she felt — her good friend was suffering from a mild passion that like a minor infection would run its course to recovery.

Andrea made the speech she had prepared, earnestly and with conviction. " . . . You're restless, that's all. Those wide-open spaces in Wyoming, I know you love them and you adore being with your children, and watching the bob-tailed deer come down to drink, and the wildflowers blooming and the pelicans doing whatever pelicans do.

But you were lonely, you didn't have enough to do. You wrote all those letters and you thought about me and you fancied yourself in love. It'll pass, you'll see. You should travel. Why don't you hop over to your Greek island?"

"Go on, teacher." Ariadne was playing with a length of red velvet ribbon that had been lying on the table. "I love to hear you talk, even when you talk rubbish."

"It's not rubbish. When you get back to town, back to Oliver, everything will be fine. And we'll meet often, we'll have good times again."

Smoothing the ribbon between her long fingers, Ariadne looked away. She had a handsome profile, a strong, hooked nose.

"I like your nose," Andrea said. "It's not often you see a real nose."

"I'm glad you like my nose. I guess that's something." She paused. "Please don't talk about my getting back to Oliver as if that would solve something. It's not Oliver I want. It's you. I don't like to talk about the two of you in the same breath."

"But you know you're crazy about him! You've often talked about —— "

Ariadne brought her hand down hard on the table, shaking teacups. "When he fucks me he gives me some pleasure. I'm human. I've got a body, and responses. But what I've said to you I've said to make you...oh hell, to throw you off the scent. I suspected you'd be wary if you knew I liked women. You're gone on men, I know that." She went on miserably, "I tried to be what you'd like — a woman who liked men. I lay low as long as I could, and then I couldn't any longer. My God, I was walking around

141

with a belly full of hot coals, thinking about you. I think about you all day and dream about you all night. I thought, I've got to tell her, and if she despises me for it it can't be any worse."

"How could I despise you! For giving me such a gift, would I despise you? In my way, I love you, you're the best friend I've ever had. But it's not in your way, you do understand, don't you, it's not in my power, there are feelings I'm not capable of. . . ."

"Ah, my love, don't be anxious, don't be sad. Tears in your eyes! That's so touching, that's worth it all, that you care so much."

"I do, I care very much. It's difficult." She creased her brow. "I can't say I wish I could be what you want me to be, because I don't. But I want to be your good friend. Ariadne? May I ask you something?"

"Have I ever loved a woman before? The answer is yes, mildly. But I've always run like a deer. I was so bloody ashamed because I wasn't normal. I decided to cure myself. I thought I had. A few casual affairs, nothing serious, but still I was there, I'd made it with a man, men liked me. Then marriage. I really did love Oliver, and I knew he was what I needed, someone strong, who'd demand all my time and attention. And the kids I adored. I still do. I like babies, they're sort of like puppies, sweet soft little things to caress and cuddle. And they grow up into neat little brats like yours and mine. Anyway — ten years of peace."

Listening, silent, Andrea kept her eyes on Ariadne's face. Only occasionally she glanced off into the dense woods beyond the garden wall.

"Sometimes I'd see a woman I liked a lot, but never enough to disturb me. No threats. Then I met you. I thought you were the most beautiful, lovely, talented woman I'd ever known, and I felt lucky, having your friendship. Maybe I was in love with you, but I didn't know it. One day I knew. It was in your apartment. You were practising and I barged in — I'd been at Zabar's, and I thought you should have some caviar too — I don't think you were overjoyed to see me, but you sweetly tried to hide that. You smiled, and as you finished playing you made some marvellous gesture with your bow. You looked triumphant and happy and other-worldly, and at the same time so luscious. All at once I knew. I saw that I'd loved you all along. I went out to the kitchen — to put the caviar on ice, I said — but really because I was doubled up in pain. That was six months ago. I've been in pain ever since. But happy too, loving you."

"Gradually you'll stop, you'll forget it ever happened. . . ."

Ariadne groaned, closing her eyes. Andrea was silent for a minute. Then she said, "Would it be easier for you if we didn't. . . if we didn't see each other for a while? I'd hate that, but it might be better, easier for you?"

"Please! A crumb is better than no bread at all. Oh, good God, look at the time. Oliver's coming up early, he'll sulk if I'm not there to greet him. He should attach me to that little boat that sails back and forth across his grandfather's grandfather clock. Then he'd always know the two things he most wants to know: what time it is and where I am." She sounded all at once cheerful, and getting up, squinting slightly against the sunlight, said, "I have an inspired idea. Teddy's away, the kids are away, come spend a night with us in town. It'd be a tremendous favour. Oliver's got a British lawyer coming and I have to help entertain him. Fact is, Oliver suggested I ask you, if that makes it any more appealing. You'll like this bloke. He's one of those long sprawly sorts with a sexy voice."

Andrea hesitated. To refuse seemed priggish. To accept seemed rash.

"Come on, say yes. A bang-up dinner and a night on the town with a couple of guys. You'll enjoy it. And I'll have pleased Oliver. Maybe in return he'll let me have my buffaloes."

They both laughed, and Andrea said yes, she would come.

The shades were drawn, the air-conditioned house faintly hummed. A bowl of lavender delphiniums stood on the piano.

"Flop." Ariadne gestured at the sofa. "Take your shoes off."

Andrea looked at her. "You're pale."

"I am? I don't feel pale. Sit down. Oliver and Desmond won't be here until seven-thirty. We have reservations at Chez Pascal for eight-thirty. We have all the time in the world. Want some iced tea? Some champers?"

"What I'd love is a shower. I might even fall asleep. I took the seven o'clock train in, and I've done a hundred errands. I bought my ma a birthday present, I've been to Patelson's, I had to go up to the apartment and...oh, it's too boring."

"You're never boring."

"I am when I talk about cockroaches and broken dishes."

"We'll go to Bloomie's tomorrow and buy you a new set of dishes."

"Ariadne, you really are pale. You're sure you feel well, you haven't got a summer virus? Why don't you take a nap?"

"What a madcap you are. Naps and showers, showers and naps."

Andrea said, uncertainly, "What do you want me to do?"

Ariadne leaned back, a hand across her eyes. "Exactly what you said."

Andrea got up, and stood there, indecisive, uncertain about Ariadne's mood. "I think I will take a shower." At the foot of the staircase she turned back. "What are you laughing at?"

"My best-laid plans. Go on up. Can you find your way to the third floor?"

The bedroom was blessedly cool. There were books on the bedtable, and on the desk another bowl of delphiniums, these of blue the colour of magnesium flame, petals tipped with a darker blue. Andrea showered, fell asleep briefly, began reading a biography of Liszt, became absorbed in it. When she looked at the clock it was half-past seven.

Oliver said she was looking particularly beautiful that evening. The British lawyer, who was indeed attractive, remarked that it was a fault peculiar to the English language that people were said to "look" beautiful. "If I were Oliver, I would have said that you *are* particularly beautiful this evening."

Ariadne lit a cigarette. "Now you've said it without having to be Oliver."

At the restaurant, Ariadne flirted with Desmond so animatedly that Andrea, with some relief, devoted her attention to Oliver. They drank a great deal of Châteaux Margaux at dinner, and later, at home, a great deal of Moët Chandon. It was after four o'clock when Desmond left, with many thanks to Ariadne and Oliver for an "absolutely marvellous" evening, and a discreetly made request of Andrea: might he have her telephone number? She said she was in the book, and counted on his head being too full of bubbles for him to remember her name.

Draping herself over the banisters, Andrea said she would never make it to the third floor.

"Stay on the second. There's plenty of room in our bed," Oliver said, tipsily adventurous.

"Always the perfect host, our Oliver." There was a glitter in Ariadne's voice.

"Goodnight, sleep well, pleasant dreams, and thank you for a lovely evening," Andrea sang out, ascending the final flight of stairs. At the top she turned, and looked back.

Ariadne was standing there motionless, her hand on the newel post, looking up at Andrea. With her lips she shaped a kiss. Andrea, smiling, blew a kiss in return, and went into the bedroom. She closed the door, glad to be alone, too fuzzy-headed to think clearly.

At a tap on the door she sat up quickly, pulling the sheet up to her shoulders.

"You rang?" Ariadne came in, smiling, carrying a breakfast tray. Her black hair was loose about her shoulders. She was barefoot and wearing a striped cotton caftan. She put the tray across Andrea's lap.

"I forgot to bring a nightgown." She wanted to get up and brush her teeth, but was embarrassed to parade about naked in front of Ariadne. Besides, she was fastidious about nakedness.

"So I see." Ariadne sat on the floor, leaning against the side of the twin bed, her head bent.

"D'you think the visiting barrister made it back to his hotel?"

"Who cares." Ariadne shrugged.

"I thought you liked him."

"The way I came on to him, you mean?" She looked up. The whites of her eyes were enormous, and milky-blue. "That was for Oliver's benefit." She picked a scrap of thread from the rug. "I decided to spend the night on the bathroom floor."

"How spartan. Why did you do that?"

"I didn't want to get into bed with him. Especially not after what he said."

"What did he say? Oh . . . that. He didn't mean it. It was a joke."

"I don't like his jokes. Anyway . . . fuck Oliver." She added, in a different tone, "No, don't ever do that. I couldn't bear it."

"But I haven't the slightest intention!" She poured coffee, and said, impatiently, "Really, Ariadne, I am not pursuing your husband."

Ariadne had sprung to her feet, facing the door. "Come in, whoever you are."

Oliver stepped in. He looked fresh, crisp, a little self-conscious. Andrea had a sudden glimpse of the schoolboy he had been, and liked him better for the glimpse.

"I came up to say good-bye."

"Good-bye, good-bye," Ariadne chanted, "Be always kind and true."

"You look very charming."

"You look very dashing," Andrea told him. "No one would believe you'd been up till all hours."

When he left, Ariadne leaned against the door, frowning. "How do you account for that? He's so innocent, he'd never . . . . I thought he was going to eat you up, beginning with your golden shoulders." She flung herself as if exhausted on the other bed, an arm over her face. The pulse in her throat fluttered frantically, gradually quieted.

Supposing her to be asleep, Andrea slipped out of bed and into the adjoining bathroom. Before emerging she wrapped herself in a bath towel.

Ariadne groaned. "Why did you cover up? God, you're beautiful. I knew you would be, but I didn't know how beautiful." She gave a short dry laugh. "No wonder Oliver was loath to leave. I love you, Andrea. I'm mad with love for you."

Keyed-up, Andrea chattered. "A friend of mine — another English bloke — once told me about a French woman he knew. She was moved to pay a call on her husband's mistress, whom she hadn't before met. They liked each other very much. When the wife was about to leave, the mistress kissed her, passionately. She'd never been kissed that way by a woman. It was the beginning of a love affair between them. They made a trio, went about together. The women thought the husband-lover didn't

know about them. One day they were on a beach — a
secluded beach — in the south of France. The husband
went off to swim, and when he came back he made love to
each of them, in turn. The wife said it was extraordinary.
She was so happy, watching her husband make love to her
friend. She said it was beautiful."

Ariadne sat up, shaking her head as if to clear from it
some frightful vision. "Are you saying you'd like Oliver to
be here, right now?"

"No, no! I thought the story would amuse you."

"It kills me. Why did you tell me?"

"I don't know! You're the one that was going on about
Oliver. It made me nervous, I suppose." She sat on the
edge of the bed, intending to get up and dress.

"I'm nervous, too. I'm shaking all over. May I sit beside
you?"

"Certainly." Andrea sat with her hands clasped tight,
her knees crossed, pressed tight together.

Ariadne stroked her arm. "I don't know what to do,
Andrea. I don't know how to go about this."

"Please! Neither do I! I don't want...I like you so
much, Ariadne, but I can't...." She swallowed, convul-
sively.

"Are you all right? You're white as a sheet. Please, lie
down. I love you. There's nothing to fear, I promise."

She sat on the mammoth bed Ariadne and Oliver shared.
Ariadne was taking things out of one handbag and putting
them in another. She seemed remote, rather sad, and did
not look at Andrea.

Andrea was astonished by what had happened, and

exhilarated. At the same time she was glad it was over, an episode previously unthinkable now safely behind. She was not chattering any more. She was talking because she wanted, out of fondness, to tell Ariadne how she had felt.

"...was going to be sick, or faint. I was terrified. I thought it would leave some visible mark on me for all the world to see, I thought my whole life would change, nothing would ever be the same again. That was when you said I was white as a sheet ———— "

"I'd better make reservations. Where would you like to have lunch?"

"Who cares, let's just find a nice cool place and wander in. Let's go to some galleries on 57th Street and have lunch over there. Or buy a sandwich and eat it in the park."

"Whatever you say."

"*Vitello tonnato* is my favourite food."

"It's very good." But Ariadne had scarcely touched it.

After a moment Andrea said quietly, though in the din she couldn't have been overheard, "You're disappointed, aren't you. It wasn't what you'd hoped. Because I couldn't. ..." She spread her hands, finding the sentence impossibly awkward, impossible to finish.

Ariadne made a sudden movement, as if to rise. "Can't we leave? It's stifling in here."

"Now you're pale. Are you all right? What a pair we are, obsessed with pallor. Do you really want to leave? You should eat something. I'm ravenous." She laughed. "Typically self-centered. You should eat because I'm ravenous. There, you're almost smiling, that's nice."

Ariadne looked down at the wineglass she was slowly

twirling. "I've got to talk to you. Do you have to take that bloody train? Couldn't you wait and drive up later? I have to wait for Oliver, dammit."

But Andrea said yes, she had to take that bloody train. She was suddenly exhausted. She could not wait to get on the train, she wanted to be alone. She had nothing more to say. She had used up all her prattle. Ariadne was like stone.

They went out into a blast of hot dirty air. The block was full of ConEd trucks, and ConEd hard-hats with drilling machines. The clatter made Andrea's head rattle, but at least it made conversation impossible. The two women swung along in step. Both had long strides, both liked walking. Now and then, to avoid being jostled, they crowded together. Out of habit, Andrea apologized each time.

Ariadne glanced at her. "Why are you sorry? I like it when you touch me. Even if it's only by accident."

"Then I won't be sorry. It's a quaint Anglo-Saxon habit, isn't it, to apologize when you accidentally touch someone."

On Madison Avenue, Andrea said, "Why don't you hop on that nice empty Number Four? It's silly for you to come all the way to the station."

"I want to come all the way to the station," Ariadne said, stubbornly, as if it were a punishment she had chosen to inflict on herself.

Andrea felt abused. She was tired too, it was hot and noisy for her too. She had done her best to keep things going, to show Ariadne how fond she was of her, to let her know that the love-making had been good and happy for her. She was sorry it had not worked out for Ariadne, but what could she do, it had not been her idea. And if now Ariadne regretted it, it was just as well.

The gates were still closed.

"Don't wait." Andrea fanned herself with a big grey Patelson's envelope.

"I want to wait." For the first time that afternoon she looked directly at Andrea. "I want to be with you every moment for the rest of my life. I love you, don't you understand? With all my heart, for ever and ever." Her voice was almost inaudible, and shaking.

All around them people were jabbering, and then pushing, as the gates opened. Caught up in the crowd, they were swept along in it.

"I didn't understand." She touched Ariadne's hand. "You seemed so remote. I thought it had been a let-down for you, I thought I was boring you. I couldn't make you talk, or laugh. . . ."

"When you're absolutely, supremely happy, when you've been reborn, do you laugh? My whole life has changed; nothing will ever be the same for me. I'd like everyone to know, I wish it did show, I wish it had left a visible mark. Your mark. I'm so proud, and so grateful." She spoke rapidly now, as if she could never get through all she had to say. "I've had to hang on to myself every minute to keep from touching you, I knew it would embarrass you, I wanted you so much at lunch I couldn't speak. But I don't want to burden you with how I feel. I want you to be happy. I want you to laugh, even if I can't, today. I love you, Andrea."

"And I do you, in my way." She was miserably aware of how meagre her words were, how cautious. She longed to be able to say more, but she could only say what she meant. Distractedly she said, "I'd better get on, or I'll have to stand all the way. I'll call you, first thing in the morning." She kissed Ariadne's cheek, and hurried into the train.

There was a vacant aisle seat. The window seat was occupied by a young woman with wispy red hair, who was eating a banana and reading *Cosmopolitan*. Sitting forward, Andrea could see Ariadne still standing there beside an empty luggage-wagon, her eyes searching the windows.

Catching her eye, Andrea smiled. Ariadne, grave faced, slightly lifted her hand. The train slid slowly along the tracks.

Andrea, looking back, saw that Ariadne was still looking at her, with the same serious preoccupied expression that she had taken for boredom or disappointment. And she knew, in a confusion of helplessness and fearfulness, that she and Ariadne were now profoundly bound together, as women, as friends, and as lovers.

A town without a graveyard

"AND THERE'S ANOTHER TYPICAL LOS ANGELES SIGHT."
There had been several on the drive from the airport,
including a papier-mâché cow straddling the sidewalk in
front of a Dari-Kween, a live elephant tethered to a striped
pole in a newly opened shopping plaza, and a traffic jam on
the other side of the freeway: miles and miles of chrome
and metal brought to a bumper-to-bumper standstill. And
now, an enormous neon-lighted black mammy with wide
white grin and polka-dotted kerchief washing clothes in a
tub atop the Atomic Age Launderette.

"For all our 'wrong-headed' ways," Mrs. Dabney said,
"you'd never see an affair like that in the South. I should
think the N.A.A.C.P. would come down on that launderette
like a ton of bricks." The black mammy, however,
reminded her of Frances, who had for twenty years been
Mrs. Dabney's mother's cook and for thirty more years
her own. Frances had recently celebrated her eighty-fifth
birthday, which event Mrs. Dabney now described.

When she had finished, Augusta said, rather pointedly,
"Do you mind if I put the radio on? I'm dying to know

how Explorer One is doing. Damn, too much static. Did you watch the blast-off on television? I did; I was absolutely riveted."

"I was on the plane, between Nashville and Houston. I believe your father was intending to watch. But do you know, Augusta, mere plane travel is something I'll never cease to marvel at. Flying around in the air like a bird, looking down at oceans and mountains and cities! I'm not certain there's any urgent need to go exploring off in space. This planet's quite mysterious enough for me."

Augusta smiled. "You're like the woman in *The Glass Menagerie*. You're so southern, Mother!"

"It's a fact I am and I wouldn't want not to be," Mrs. Dabney said, good-humouredly. "So are you, honey."

"I was born in the South," Augusta conceded. "But it wasn't my choice and I don't consider myself a southerner."

"Your roots are southern."

"Roots! People who need them are insecure. You won't hear any talk about roots in Desert Gap."

At Riverside they stopped in a Frostee-Tastee, Augusta having remembered that her mother was addicted to a mid-morning Coca-Cola. The Frostee-Tastee was shaped like an inverted ice-cream cone, and the employees wore cone-shaped paper hats. "What'll it be, girls?" asked the youth behind the counter, snapping his fingers to the beat of *Never on Sunday*, which was blaring from the juke-box. Mrs. Dabney said she would have a lime Coke. Augusta said coldly that she would have a glass of ice-water. She did not appreciate being addressed as "girl", and soft drinks she shunned because they were bad for the teeth.

Mrs. Dabney had taken off her white gloves and placed them on top of her alligator bag. Augusta studied her mother's reflection in the looking-glass on the opposite wall. Small, elegant rather than stylish, with an animated face still pretty in her late sixties (Augusta had been what her mother called "the sweet surprise" of her mid-forties), she had delicate features and a pair of fine dark eyes. These eyes Augusta had inherited. Otherwise she was, as people said, her father's daughter.

Mrs. Dabney's southern speech had caught the ear of the young woman seated next to her, who wore a bulging pink sweater, matching pink plastic rollers in her blonde hair and long fake eyelashes. The young woman said that she just loved southern accents. She herself came from Minnesota and lived with her husband and three kids in a trailer park. Augusta listened tolerantly as her mother elicited information from her new acquaintance, and then glancing at the clock — which was numbered not with digits but with blobs of ice cream, each a different colour — pointed out that they should go on.

They drove very fast along the road that ran between the February-green hills. They had left the city smog behind them and the air was brilliant; ahead of them the San Bernardino mountains lifted frosted peaks into the high blue. As they turned off the white-topped highway that rolled sleekly into Palm Springs, Augusta slowed down.

"Now we're coming to the real desert. It's like nothing you've ever seen before." She gazed with pride and satisfaction, as if she had had a hand in the making of it, at the exotic country through which they were driving. Grey-green plains prickled with sage and cactus spread off to the hills that ringed the valley. The dazzling desert light lent to everything a graphic quality — vivid and absolutely new as if it had just been constructed, perhaps of papier mâché like the red and white cow at the Dari-Kween. The mountains were of the same bold craftsmanship. Clothed in skins of brick-red and ochre and burnt sienna, striped with shadows, carelessly creased and folded, they might have been great prehistoric animals lumbering across a sky which had that morning been painted aquamarine.

Ascending, they reached a plateau and came in sight of another range of mountains — these jagged and pointed like the drip-castles children build on the seashore.

Augusta brought the car to a stop, and gestured. "What do you think of *that*?"

Mrs. Dabney said, "Why, it certainly is striking. Though perhaps a little barbaric."

"You ought to be pleased then. It bears out your theory. When I told you we were going to move out here you said Southern California was 'beyond civilization'."

"But I didn't expect the countryside to look so fierce. Of course, it is desert, it's not where people would normally choose to live. Those high mountains are quite handsome, though I confess I prefer mountains to tower over trees and lakes, not just stick up in that barren way. Speaking of barren, I hope you've started a garden? Those pictures you sent at Christmas made me downright depressed. Sue felt it too. She wondered how you could stand it."

Augusta thought of her eldest sister's white pillared house in its Belle Meade setting of cropped lawns and well-trained trees and prettily appointed flower borders. "Good old Sue. What would she and Henry say if those tax-dollars they're always complaining about were spent putting up fancy houses for physicists to live in?"

"That's what I told her. I said it was only temporary and when you and David go back to Princeton you'll have a real home again. But meantime a garden can make a world of difference. The meanest little place looks better with something blossoming around it."

"I'd scarcely call our house 'mean'. But if you want blossoms around it you're welcome to plant them. And then tie them down so they won't blow away. I don't have time to fuss with gardens. I'm too busy with Adam."

"Needless to say! But I wish you had a little help with him. Sue and Kate would be lost without household help. Not that I don't admire the way you manage, all on your own. Still, you may find when you have more children. . . . "

"I won't find that I need help with my children. I totally disapprove of women who turn their children over to some ignoramus for the most important years of their lives." Augusta spoke in her most austere manner. "David and I intend to have another child in four years. We'll probably be back east by then, and when he — or she — is in a really good nursery school, I'll get a degree in architecture. I've become very interested in low-cost urban housing."

"Urban renewal, and the like?"

"D'you know what the victims of urban renewal programs call it? 'Urban removal.' It's one of those malapropisms that hits the nail right on the head." She pulled up again. They had reached the top of the pass: the road ahead ribboned down around curves in the hills to the plain below, which was guarded by mountains. To the north there was a gap in the range, through which could be seen a wash of blue sky.

"And that" — Augusta gestured to the town beneath them — "is Desert Gap. Take a good look. It's your first sight of the brave new world."

Mrs. Dabney leaned forward for a better view. "Why it looks like a dollhouse town! And just think of all the important things going on down there, atom bombs being made, and all those dreadful new inventions for killing people."

Augusta said, indulgently, "They're not inventing new ways to kill people. They're inventing a better world for people to live in. And the atom bomb is practically obsolete."

"Is it really?" Mrs. Dabney sounded interested, admiring, untroubled. These matters, she implied, were important but beyond her immediate interest. Her immediate interest was and always had been people. "And you know, I still don't understand exactly what David does. I know he's a physicist, but when people ask me what he does as a physicist I'm at a loss to say."

"He sits and thinks. He's always liked to sit and think — now he gets paid for it."

"And what does he think about?"

"Spin-waves. My chief rival: the spin-wave."

"It sounds right fascinating. What a lot I shall be learning."

"The first thing you must learn," Augusta said in the firm, kind voice she might have used with a child, "is not to ask a lot of questions. I wouldn't dream of asking David exactly what they're doing at the Mesa. That's the Mesa." She pointed at the group of buildings, in the bright light a gleaming white blur, that lay to the north of the town. "We'll never get beyond the gates, of course...why are you laughing?"

"Smiling, honey, merely smiling. I was thinking, What a change in Augusta! I remember how you used to scold me for not being more interested in your father's law practice. Southern women were no better than pets, you said, and you'd come home from Vassar for vacations and ask your father learned questions about banking law, and argue with him about capitalism, and lecture me about women keeping up with their husband's interests, and I remember saying you'd better marry a man whose interests were interesting to you. And you've married one whose interests are so interesting you're not allowed to keep up with them." She put a soft hand on Augusta's. "Don't be offended, please. I'm only teasing. I think you're a wonderful young woman, and David's a wonderful young man and I'm happy as any lark to be here with you. Goodness, what are those grotesque-looking things, all legs and arms?"

"Joshua trees. Stunning, aren't they."

"Perhaps I'll get used to them. Did I write to you about the old tulip tree and how it came crashing down in that December ice-storm? I wept, seeing it. When they sawed it up and hauled it away I went out to look at where it had been. There was nothing but the poor raw stump. But all at once I could see that fine tree rising above me, all green foliage and sunlight and birds twittering in it. You used to love to sit in it and read." She laughed — she had a charming laugh. "Do you remember when the Garden Club was coming to tea and you stole a Lady Baltimore cake that Frances had just baked, and you invited the Peyton children over and you all went up in the tree with the cake —— "

"And Tim Peyton dropped it. We brushed the dirt off it and ate it anyway."

"Did you know that Tim turned Catholic and joined that silent order of monks? The family was mortified — the Peytons have been Episcopalians for ever. Tim was such a lively boy — to think of him shut up in a place where no one says a blessed word all day long! Away up north too. I believe it's in Rhode Island."

"He probably got tired of hearing his mother talk. She talked more than anyone in Nashville except crazy old Miss Ida-Belle who kept a hundred cats so she'd have someone to talk to. Oh, how I used to resent it when after parties you'd send me over there with a hamper of food. I know it hurt her pride."

"But she liked delicacies. And Coca-Cola. When she died a few years ago they found the whole cellar full of Coke bottles, all neatly stacked away. She must have collected them for years. I suppose it gave her some pleasure." She laughed.

Augusta did not laugh, thinking instead of Miss Ida-Belle, of all the pitiable or eccentric people on the charitable Dabney payroll or on the long list of friends and kinfolk on whom time and energy and money and thought had to be spent. To her mother, the assumption of such obligations gave purpose and value to life, but to Augusta the obligations were in themselves immoral, the price that had to be paid in the South for its absorption in the past, its paternalistic system, its passion for the personal, and its absurd and inefficient caste system.

They were skimming along, approaching the town with its rows of identical houses painted in pastel colours: desert pink, lemon yellow, robin's egg blue, mint green. They entered on Fifth Avenue, crossed A Street, B Street, C Street. "It goes straight through the alphabet," Augusta explained. "It couldn't be a simpler town plan — avenues numbered, streets alphabetized. Even a nitwit couldn't get lost."

"But surely a nitwit would never come here?"

"You never know. One might come to visit." Augusta glanced at her mother and they both laughed.

The houses stretched in neat rows on either side of the wide streets, each fronted by a rectangular patch of lawn, each backed by a bricked-in patio and fenced in bamboo. The morning sun splashed against picture windows. Mrs. Dabney said, dubiously, "Why, it looks just like a development."

"It is a development." Augusta explained that people in Desert Gap were amused, not apologetic about the uniformity of the town. It made Desert Gap seem a satire on tract-house existence, and a good joke on sociologists who were alarmed at the contemporary American fear of nonconformity. For here, where streets were alphabetized and avenues numbered, where houses and backyards were identical, where badges were worn and passes carried, where everything was government owned, individuality flourished.

As if to provide an example there emerged at that moment from a sage-green house a corpulent man in wrinkled khaki pants and an old Norfolk jacket. His hair was like a clown's wig, a thicket of grey and black, and he wore heavy horn-rimmed spectacles. Mounting a bicycle he hunched over the handlebars and rode recklessly off down the middle of the street.

"And is he a scientist?"

"A mathematician. His name is Oertel, he's a genius. He lives in that house with scarcely a stick of furniture. He hasn't a family. Now and then he flies off to London or Stockholm to lecture, carrying a toothbrush and a pair of pajamas in the pocket of his raincoat. All that he needs he carries in his head. He's the only person I've ever known who's really free, not tied to possessions or people or places. If you ask him for a meal you have to go and get him, otherwise he forgets to come. And he doesn't talk very much — he's quite likely to smile gently and nod off to sleep. When he does talk he's marvellous. He'll start out by saying something like 'I do not know much about your Shackspeare,'" — she imitated Oertel's heavy accent — "and then he'll proceed to absolutely illuminate Shakespeare. Sometimes he borrows a fiddle and plays in David's chamber-music group."

"He puts me in mind of Harland Ware, in Charleston."

"Oh, Mother," Augusta wailed, "Harland Ware is a mere dilettante!" Harland Ware played the fiddle and painted landscapes; for years he had been translating the *Odyssey*. The fact that he had never finished it did not mean a thing in Charleston. People said, Such a brilliant man! He's translating Homer. "Don't you see, people here are different. They get things done, what they do matters." It was probably a waste of breath to try to explain. Her mother would not see the difference between Harland Ware and Oertel—she would think of them both, respectfully, as learned.

"But where is my precious Adam?" asked disappointed Mrs. Dabney, when she came into the silent house.

"He's spent the morning with a playpen-mate on R Street. That's the way we work it here. We have an infant-and-child-care cooperative arrangement. It's super. Much better than having a baby-sitter who does nothing anyway but gawk at the tube. And babies love to play with other babies. You have a little rest. I'll go get Adam."

"He certainly looks well cared for!" Mrs. Dabney was ecstatic about her grandson. Beautiful, she pronounced him, and very advanced for seven months. She couldn't believe that since October he had grown so big and strong and intelligent; he would be walking and talking in no time.

Adam was delighted with his grandmother. He stood there on her lap, sturdy little bare feet firmly planted, examining with plump delicate fingers her eyes, her pearls, her hair. She danced him up and down. He laughed, showing two pearl-like teeth.

"He's the perfect image of his grandfather. Except for the eyes—those are definitely David's, those great blue eyes. I think, after all, that his name suits him. When he was a tiny baby it seemed rather formal. Where did the name Adam come from?"

"From the Bible."

Mrs. Dabney thought that a good joke on herself. "I meant, there'd never been an Adam in the family. I thought perhaps it was in David's family."

"No, we named him for himself." It had been her idea to name this boy, born in Desert Gap, for the first man. She had not told anyone that, except David. It could have been interpreted as cute or precious or even romantic, and a romantic was the last thing Augusta wanted to be.

"Your father is overjoyed, having a grandson. The first male child in two generations! I had only daughters, your sisters have only daughters, so I suppose Adam is all the more appropriate for him, though I'm sure you weren't thinking of that. You'll bring him home again, soon, won't you? It's difficult for your father to get away, except on a flying visit, in winter. Next summer, perhaps? The heat here will be intolerable."

Augusta thought of the cool wind that always sprang up under the desert sky, of the white light of the moon lying full on the plain and the mountains, and of the silence of a desert night. True, the days were hot, but all the houses were air conditioned and in the late afternoon everyone gathered at the community pool. She remembered the jungle heat of southern summers, fern-hung streams and brackish ponds steaming under the heavy yellow eye of the sun, motionless foliage and borders of hot-looking red and pink flowers, fans whirring in the torpid air, whippoorwill calling at dusk, the thrumming of peepers and cicadas. Such *busy* sounds: nothing was ever silent. She remembered too the idleness and frivolity of her growing-up years — the country-club life, endless flirting and sweet-talk, and gossip, gossip, gossip. Not for her a southern summer.

"Sue and Kate would love to have you at Nags Head. Officially, you know, the house is as much yours as theirs, and with a family coming along it's going to be very nice for you and David and your children to have that big old house to visit every summer. There's no air like the Carolina sea air. The desert air is said to be bracing, but it's ruinous to the complexion. Here it is, only February, and you're already as brown as a pecan pie."

"Some people like pecan pies." Who but her mother, brought up on all that magnolia-petal imagery, would criticize rather than compliment her? Augusta rejoiced in her smooth brown skin. It gave her a sense of well-being. And her short fair hair, bleached by the sun, had platinum streaks in it. Her mother, being southern, thought "white" skin a sign of God's favour. To provoke, Augusta said, "The most beautiful skin colour I've ever seen was on Frances's granddaughter, Betty Jean. She looked like taffy. Plenty of 'white' blood in that family though I'm sure no white man ever owned up to it. She was my best friend. The first time Frances brought her to our house she said to me, 'Is you mah cousin?' and I said, 'Yes, Ah is,' and we kissed and hugged and after that she came every day. Then of course she went to her separate but far from equal school and I went to my superior school and that was that. I wonder what's happened to her. I suppose she's scrubbing somebody's floors for a dollar an hour."

Unruffled, Mrs. Dabney said, "She graduated from Howard University four years ago, and she's teaching school in Boston. All I meant, honey, is that if you don't protect your skin you'll age before your time."

"I really don't care how I look when I'm forty. What

difference will it make, then? This is how I choose to look now." She bent to take Adam off for his lunch. Her mother's face, close up, was silken. Well, that was her style. Augusta herself preferred something more striking.

"And here is David home!" Mrs. Dabney rose to greet her son-in-law, arms outstretched.

"Welcome to Number Thirty-Eight P Street, Miss Ellen. You look terrific."

"I'm the better for seeing you. Not to mention Augusta and that gorgeous boy of yours. You look wonderfully well, handsome as ever. And your beard—Augusta wrote about it—it's very becoming. It's a pity they went out of fashion."

"I think they've been back a while," said Augusta drily. "I suppose they haven't caught on in Nashville."

David went off to make drinks. Not the usual California jug-wine this evening: Augusta's father had sent two quarts of Jack Daniels. Lifting his glass, David toasted first his mother-in-law and then his wife.

She ought to be glad, Augusta knew, that her husband and mother got along so well: no dreary mother-in-law jokes in her house. But sometimes it went too far. She felt left out, and this made her perverse. She argued against everything they agreed upon. Dickens was not her favourite novelist; she thought Gilbert and Sullivan trivial; Bob Hope bored her. And so forth. She picked up a book and began to read when her mother entertained David with family tales, or anecdotes about Augusta as a little girl, or long drawn-out stories about people he had never met. All these David found, or pretended to find, absorbing. And

he liked her mother's cosseting of him and the attentions
she paid him because he was a man. All the southern ways
that exasperated Augusta seemed to charm him. "Miss
Ellen" — which was what her other sons-in-law called her,
and young friends and of course servants — David had
taken up as a kind of joke, and it had stuck. He now used it
as if he were a southerner born and bred, one of an
immense extended family of sisters and cousins and uncles
and aunts, rather than an only child, now orphaned, born
and bred in Nebraska.

David's father, a Scottish immigrant, had been a school-
teacher. His mother had taught piano. Both parents had
been very ambitious for this son who had begun reading,
and playing piano, when he was three years old, and at a
very young age had taken to speculating about the universe. (His mother had kept a journal about him, which
was now a treasured possession of Augusta's. When he
was seven, she had asked him what he was thinking about,
and he had answered, "I was thinking, if I were God, what
would I have started with?") His father had died of cancer
when David was ten; his mother had died two years before
he had graduated *summa cum laude* from M.I.T. It seemed to
Augusta cruel as well as sad that the mother who had
dedicated her life to her son should have died before
knowing how brilliantly he had fulfilled his early promise.

All the while that David, in a four-square shingled
house on the Nebraska prairies, was being propelled into
his future, Augusta in a polished shadowy old house in
Nashville was being drawn back into the past, being taught
to model herself on past generations of women, being

nourished on memory and myth, being conditioned to feel rather than think. She had once heard it said that southerners think with their emotions and feel with their intellects. That had made a deep impression on her, for she did not want to be like that. She wanted to escape, to be free in a place where people lived for ideas. Vassar had seemed to her just such a golden place and she had broken family tradition and gone north to college. It amused her now to think of her naïvety, dreaming in such fashion of Vassar. It was of Desert Gap she had really been dreaming.

Her mother, she supposed, would find it a barren place, as barren of personal histories as of trees. She had a passion for giving everyone a family and a history. She loved connections, coincidences, she relished the accidental. Augusta preferred to view life as a series of decisions freely arrived at, and was willing to take the consequences of any decision she had made. Her mother saw in everyone's life the workings of an inexorable fate. This did not make her gloomy or piously resigned. On the contrary it filled her with a zest for life in its unpredictability and complexity. The lives of perfectly humdrum people took on in her telling a fictional quality, while she spoke of fictional characters as if they were old friends with whom she had grown up.

"Honestly, she can make Oedipus sound like a boy from Nashville," Augusta had once complained to David, who had replied, "Well, he was just a small-town kid." (Her mother had described Oedipus as "that unfortunate young man who inadvertently married his own mother.")

In the morning Mrs. Dabney asked if she might borrow

the car for an hour or so. She wanted to go on a shopping expedition. She was certain she could find her way around town.

"Still, I think I'd better drive you," Augusta said. "It's a stick-shift. You wouldn't be able to work it."

Amused, Mrs. Dabney said, "Honey, I was driving a stick-shift long before you were born. I learned on your grandfather's old Packard touring car." Augusta tried to picture her mother as a flapper, zipping around Nashville in a Packard touring car.

Well pleased, Mrs. Dabney returned. She had found without any trouble the Desert Gap Nursery Gardens, and there had run into another customer, "a very intelligent young man", who had advised her about seedlings and bedding plants and ground-covers. The young man had cousins in Shelbyville — she had promised to look them up when next she was there. "I go at least once a month to visit Cousin Virginia Tucker. Poor old dear, her mind wanders but she does love company." The name of the young man? It was a Jewish name. She thought a moment. "Abe Gottlieb."

Abe Gottlieb was David's boss, head of the T group. There was a story about Abe and his twin brother who had graduated the same year from Princeton. Abe was at the top of the class with an average of 99.9 per cent. He was known as "the smart Gottlieb". His brother, whose average was 99.6 per cent, was known as "the dumb Gottlieb".

"All the same," Mrs. Dabney said, on hearing this, "he was exceedingly pleasant. He knows a great deal about gardening. And he introduced me to a perfectly charming little lemon tree. It bears sweet lemons, and I had them plant it in a handsome redwood tub. They'll deliver it this afternoon. Mr. Gottlieb offered to bring it, but I wouldn't hear of it. I suppose he finds gardening relaxing after thinking so much all day."

"Thinking's a game to him. Maybe he does know all about gardening. He knows all about everything. But the fact is he doesn't have a garden. He had gravel laid in his backyard to keep the weeds down. For relaxation he plays the bongo drums. He's terrific on the bongo drums." She was very glad to be able to put that in; it would be unendurable if her mother started telling her about people in Desert Gap.

Knowing that her mother would expect some sort of social event in her honour, Augusta proposed a tea-party. Mrs. Dabney said Augusta must not go to any trouble for her. All the same, the silver tea-service, a wedding present never before used, suddenly appeared stripped of its lemon-yellow wrappings and polished to a white bright-ness. Augusta called about thirty women of varying ages, and self-consciously explained that she was giving a tea for her mother. She half expected them to hoot with laughter — a ladies' tea party in Desert Gap, what a quaint notion! But everyone came, and talked and laughed and ate rolled watercress sandwiches and wafer-thin brown bread and tiny lemon tarts with fluted golden edges and pecan puffs. Everyone said how nice it was to go to a pretty party for women only instead of the usual noisy cocktail, and everyone told Augusta that her mother was absolutely charming. A darling, they said, or, Such a lady, or, I'm crazy about the way she talks. One woman, for whose mind Augusta had the greatest respect, actually spoke of "gracious living", a term Augusta would never have used and had never expected to hear from the lips of someone who was married to a mathematician and herself translated mathematical textbooks from Russian.

In the course of the afternoon, Mrs. Dabney accepted many invitations to morning coffee, lunch, or tea. She was not in the least offended when Augusta said she was too busy to waste hours socializing. "There's no earthly reason for you to trail about with your mother."

Her tone was so equable that Augusta only said, "You'll have a much better time without me. You can really dig in, get the lowdown on everyone."

Predictably, Mrs. Dabney was soon possessed of several life-histories and one or two secret sorrows. In these her daughter pretended not to be interested. "What matters to me," she said, "is what people are, what they do, what they're making of themselves, never mind if their mothers were alcoholic or their first husbands ran off with their best friends."

"Augusta, honey...." Mrs. Dabney seemed hesitant. "Sometimes I think you've become just a little priggish. The sort of person, don't you know, who prefers a lecture to a conversation?"

Before Augusta, stung by the word "priggish", could think of a suitably withering reply, her mother went on, "The oddest thing about this town I just found out today. Do you realize there's not a graveyard in Desert Gap? Fancy a town without a place for the dead. It doesn't seem real, somehow."

"Why would we need a graveyard? There aren't any dead people. Don't you think it would be a little disconcerting for people to come to a new town and find that the planners had thoughtfully laid out a cemetery? With a door prize, maybe, for the first occupant. A marble angel blowing on a trumpet, or a stone urn full of flowers. What an odd thing to worry about."

"I'm not worried. I merely wondered what you would do if someone died."

"Bury him, of course. As a matter of fact, someone did die, just after we came here. A maintenance man, at the Mesa. Something blew up. It was all very hush-hush, of course."

"And where was he buried?" Mrs. Dabney asked, bright with interest.

"He was sent home. To wherever he'd come from."

"I see."

Sometimes Augusta didn't know if her mother was shrewdly making a point or just rambling on. "I never denied, did I, that except for the children born here everyone comes from somewhere else? I only said it didn't matter."

When she told David about the conversation, he kissed her, and said, "Sweetie, if a Californian went to the South, the first thing he'd find lacking would be backyard swimming pools. It's a cultural difference, that's all."

"Yes, but she managed to make it sound significant. As if Desert Gap were a fantasy town, a kind of high-toned Disneyland where everyone's deluded."

"You read too much into what she says. I think she's having a hell of a good time here. She wasn't criticizing, just remarking."

"I met a neighbour of yours today," Mrs. Dabney said later, when they were at dinner. "Mr. Thomas Patterson, at Number Eight. Adam wanted to hold my postcards — I'd bought a dozen showing those gates to the Mesa that I'm never going to get beyond — and then the little rascal threw them away, and in the wind they blew all over someone's front lawn. As I was picking them up, Mr. Patterson happened to return home, and very kindly helped me. And — this is the remarkable fact — the minute I saw him, even before I heard his name, I knew I'd seen him before. Then when he told me his name I said, 'Why Tom Patterson, I knew I'd seen you before. I was Ellen Tucker in those days, and I lived in Nashville and it must be almost fifty years since we met.' He looked at me, very polite, but blank, as if I'd made a mistake. The odd thing was not that he'd forgotten a young girl named Ellen Tucker whom he might possibly have seen at dances years earlier, but that he'd forgotten that he lived in Nashville a year! I didn't press the point. But I'd take an oath on the Bible that he's the Tom Patterson I casually knew all those years ago. What do you make of that?"

"Mistaken identity?" David suggested.

"No, there was no mistake about it."

"Does he have some tell-tale identifying mark that you recognized?" Augusta asked, teasingly. "A V-shaped scar over his right eyebrow?"

"Nothing like that. It was his face, and his bearing. Well! It's right interesting. I'd like to meet his wife. She wasn't at the tea, was she. I believe she was away at the time. I gather it's a second marriage for her."

"How exactly did you 'gather' that?" asked Augusta.

"Did you ask him how many times his wife had been married?"

"It came naturally into the conversation, honey. He spoke of having a grandson Adam's age, then said it was actually his wife's grandson. He was very admiring of Adam, and spoke so highly of David. Of you too, Augusta. His words were 'Beauty and Brains: an unbeatable combination.' I quite agreed with him. What does Mr. Patterson do? Or is that a forbidden question?"

"He's in administration. Budget department," David said. "A nice guy, Tom Patterson."

"He has a striking face. You wouldn't forget it."

"Oh . . ." cried Augusta. "I know who you took him for — Father's cousin, Curtiss Dabney. I noticed that too. Their faces look carved out of granite. When they smile, it's a surprise. You don't expect those faces to smile. And they're both enormously tall."

"They always did look alike," Mrs. Dabney said. "Once, at a dance, there was an embarrassment when Tom was taken for Curtiss."

"What you ought to do," Augusta spoke sarcastically, "is run right down to his house and confront him. Tell him you know he comes from Nashville and if he doesn't admit it you'll sick the F.B.I. on him. That'll bring him to his knees."

"He didn't come from Nashville. He was just there for a spell. There's Adam, fussing in his crib, poor lamb. Just this once, may I pick him up?"

Mrs. Dabney said no more about Tom Patterson. She seemed willing to drop the subject — perhaps seeing that her insistence on it grated on Augusta — and would probably have done so if Betsy Perkins hadn't come back, that week, to Desert Gap.

Betsy lived at the other end of P Street. Her husband was a biochemist on leave from Columbia. She was in her forties and had an attractive, rather craggy face, and unusual turquoise eyes. She and Augusta had in common a great liking for New York and Ingmar Bergman films. An accomplished pianist, she owned a fine Steinway, and chamber-music enthusiasts, including David, often gathered of an evening in her pink house. Augusta enjoyed those gatherings, though they made her wish that she had not sulked and scowled her way through three years of piano lessons instead of practising.

They had known each other for three or four months before Augusta learned that Betsy also came from the South. Certainly she had left behind all traces of her native Savannah speech. She had gone north to boarding-school and college, and after her marriage had continued to live in New York. Apparently she had money of her own — she was always flying back East to visit her two sons at Harvard, and go to concerts and opera.

She had been away when Mrs. Dabney arrived — no answer when Augusta had called her about the tea — and then one morning they ran into one another at the Desert Gap market. Betsy was buying filet mignon and enormous snow-white mushrooms and French wine. Her husband, she said, had been living on TV dinners and canned chili, and deserved a decent meal. "Why don't you and David come over tomorrow evening? I'll nab some other people and we'll play."

"Lovely," Augusta said, and at once her conscience

spoke up. Her mother would dearly love to meet Betsy.
"...so perhaps you'd come to tea? I warn you, she'll talk
your ear off about Savannah. She knows hundreds of
people there. She probably knows your whole family. Can
you stand talking southern for a while?"

When Augusta brought in the tea tray, her mother turned
to her and said in a tone of mixed reproach and excitement, "All these months you've lived practically next door
to Betsy Perkins, and you never did find out that she was
Betsy Todd."

Augusta gave Betsy a what-did-I-tell-you smile.

"The Todds were dear friends of your great-uncle
Reynolds Tucker and your great-aunt Charlotte. In fact,
Uncle Rennie was Julia Todd's godfather. Betsy's mother's
godfather! Which makes us all some kind of kin. Fancy not
finding that out."

Pouring tea, Augusta said, "The first question I ask
people isn't usually who was their mother's godfather."

"Oh, put that way...." Mrs. Dabney laughed.

"I don't think we talked much about our families, did
we, Augusta. Somehow people don't, out here. Life seems
very transient in Desert Gap. It's a company town — we're
here because there's a job to be done. I suppose it'll all
crumble away like those old mining towns. There'll be
nothing left but a heap of radioactive rubble. I don't share
the optimism prevalent here. I think it will someday be
known as The Place Where the End of the World was
Invented." She smiled at Augusta. "You look shocked. It's
true, I don't often talk that way around here."

Augusta went to the kitchen to get juice for Adam.

When she came back, Betsy was saying, "...sometimes I long for the sight of a live oak all dripping with Spanish moss."

Who would have thought Betsy would succumb so quickly to the southern party-line? Or would actually say, deliberately drawling it out, "Miz Dabney, this fudge cake is *sin*fully rich"?

Adam liked the cake too. He rubbed chocolate-coated fingers on his adoring grandmother's dress; sat on Betsy's lap while she played This Little Piggie on his toes. The conversation between the two women flowed around Augusta, murmurous and vivacious at once. Nothing of consequence was being said, nothing witty, nothing vital, but it all conveyed a sense of ease and comfort. Augusta thought, this is what a woman's life once was: generations, connections between them.

A car door slammed. She heard David's voice and another male voice that she did not recognize, and was for an instant disconcerted when Tom Patterson — stooping slightly through the doorway — preceded David into the room. If her mother said one word about Nashville....

Tom's car had broken down and he had hitched a ride with David. There were the usual pleasantries. David said it was great to have Betsy back and when could they play the Dvořák E-flat? He'd been working on it. Tom wanted to know where Betsy had been, spoke with mock disapproval of "restless women". "My wife barely touched down last month. Our daughter's being married this weekend in Chicago. Sally's up there sewing bridesmaids' dresses and planning feasts. I have the easy part — I foot the bill and I get to give the bride away."

"I didn't know you had a daughter," Betsy said.

"She's Sally's daughter — bourbon on the rocks for me, David, I stay away from harmful substances like water — but I like to think of her as mine too. I married late in life and acquired a family along with my wife."

"Labour saving," Betsy said.

Mrs. Dabney seemed not to be listening. She was playing peek-a-boo with Adam, who laughed so hard that he fell over and bumped his head. He bellowed. There was a small commotion.

When Adam was soothed, Betsy got up. She must fly, she said. "Dvořák tomorrow evening," she promised David. Embracing Mrs. Dabney, she invited her to lunch the next day. "We've had the most marvellous time," she told Tom and David. "We've been doing what Augusta calls talking southern."

David put an arm around Augusta. "Did you reminisce about Nashville, you and your mother and Betsy?"

"You from Nashville, Betsy?" Tom asked, with polite interest.

"No, are you? You say Nashv'lle like a native."

Augusta started, hearing that, and glanced at Tom.

"I have a sharp ear. I noted the way Mrs. Dabney said it the other day. And of course I've heard Augusta say it any number of times."

When have I talked about Nashville, Augusta wondered, and for a moment almost believed that Tom had, after all, a part in her mother's scenario. But there he stood, affable, untroubled, gazing benevolently down at Adam, who was attempting to untie his shoelaces. It had been a friendly remark, nothing more. It made it seem as if they were good friends, rather than neighbours who in fact did not know each other very well.

He finished his drink and left shortly after Betsy. Mrs. Dabney, shaking hands with him, said it had been a pleasure to see him again, and wished him a happy time at the wedding. She did not say a word about Nashville.

She waited until they were at dinner to do that. She took up her theme as if it had never been interrupted. "Betsy noticed it right off — she was quicker than I was. But then it didn't strike me as it did her. I knew he'd lived in Nashville a full year. That's long enough to pick up a habit."

Augusta shook her head, portentously. "Mother, you're becoming obsessed. That's what you are — obsessed about Tom Patterson. Look, he's an honest man. He wouldn't be in Desert Gap if he weren't. D'you think our beloved F.B.I. — if you'll pardon my using that expression again — would have cleared him if there'd been anything unsavoury in his past?"

"Such as that he'd lived in Nashville for a year?" David asked.

"Very funny." Augusta gave him a look.

"Perhaps the F.B.I. knew perfectly well that he'd lived in Nashville and attended Vanderbilt. Surely that wouldn't be a black mark on his record," Mrs. Dabney said.

Augusta affected incredulity. "You mean you don't think he's a spy? You don't think we should have him liquidated immediately?"

"Of course I don't think he's a spy. I think he's a very nice man who for reasons of his own doesn't care to remember that he lived in Nashville. Or doesn't care to talk about it." And after one of those pregnant pauses in which all good raconteurs specialize, she added, "After today, I think it's as well that he doesn't."

"I will not ask what you mean by that!" Augusta turned to David. "Tell me what you did today."

He grinned wickedly. "I can't. It's a secret."

Furious, she said, "I'm the only person here that doesn't have a secret! And doesn't want one!"

Only David's contrite apologies for teasing, her mother's for "going on" about Tom Patterson, calmed her temper.

They were going to a party that evening, on J Street. Mrs. Dabney insisted on doing the dishes. "You two run along and enjoy yourselves. Augusta, why don't you bring me that dress that needs hemming. I noticed yesterday it shows where you've pinned it up."

Augusta fetched the dress, and while she was at it, several skirts with missing hooks or pinned-up hems, and shirts of David's that needed buttons sewn on. Dropping them on the sofa, she said to David, "when I was little I was taught that the most appalling fate that could befall me was to be in an accident when I had a pin in my panties or my vest, or anywhere in my clothes. What would the nurses say, and the doctors, and the ambulance men who picked up my poor smashed little body, if they saw a pin in my underwear?"

"I imagine they'd wash their hands of such a person."

Mrs. Dabney laughed. "It does seem ridiculous in retrospect, a little thing like a pin mattering so much." She added, in a different tone, "We did put a great deal of stock in appearances."

"Which as we all know can be deceiving. As in the case of...." Within Augusta, pride struggled against curiosity, and lost. She said, as if casually, "So what's the scoop on Tom Patterson? Who d'you think he really is?"

"I'll tell you who he is," Mrs. Dabney said composedly. "He's Betsy Perkins' father. He doesn't know that, of course."

"I truly think she's going dotty," Augusta told David, as they swung along Eighth Avenue. "Maybe she has some rare form of desert fever. Now she's got Betsy Perkins mixed up in her Nancy Drew case. Having claimed a few hours ago that she knew Betsy's parents intimately, she's produced another one." She stopped, lifting her head and gazing about. "Oh, that moonlight! The shadows so deep and black, and then all the whiteness. Let's sleep out some full-moon night. I used to believe that if you slept in the full moonlight you'd go loony. I was so scared I used to draw the shades and pull the covers up over my head. You see what a ridiculous upbringing I had? The horrors of going mad in the moonlight, having an accident in a pin, and all the tales.... But I'm simply going to ignore this one. I won't mention it to her again."

"That's the spirit. Don't let it bother you."

"It doesn't bother you? An announcement like that? Just—bang—that man down the street is the father of that woman up the street, but of course he doesn't know it."

"Suppose it's true. What difference would it make?"

She faced him, accusatory. "You believe it, don't you."

"Oh, 'believe'," he said, rather disparagingly. "It's not a

matter of belief. Facts are facts." He slowed his steps —
they were on J Street, approaching their friend's house.
"For what it's worth, Tom did go to Vanderbilt for a year.
He once mentioned it. It was just in passing. A slip, I
suppose. I'd forgotten about it until today. It came up in
connection with the Scopes trial. Monkey business." He
kissed her. "Laugh. That was a joke."

"Then why did he lie to my mother? And to Betsy,
today?"

"He didn't lie. He just said he had a sharp ear."

"He implied a lie, which is equally immoral. Why
didn't you challenge him?"

"Sweetie, you wouldn't have liked that one bit, would
you. Why force a showdown? It's not as if it were a
professional matter. It's entirely personal. A chapter in his
life he prefers to leave unread. Maybe I would too, if
somewhere along the line I'd spawned a kid and then
vamoosed."

Abe Gottlieb was at the party, with his bongo drums.
He wanted to know how her lemon tree was doing, and
her creeping thyme and rose geraniums, and the mint her
mother had brought in a plastic bag from her backyard in
Nashville. One of these days he was going to come by and
get some. He said that now he knew where Augusta had
come by her good looks. Augusta resolved not to pass the
compliment on — she was too vexed with her mother.
Besides, she did not look at all like her mother, except for
her eyes, any more than Betsy Perkins looked like her
so-called father. Then a very displeasing image of those
two faces presented itself: she saw in Betsy's a female
version of Tom's.

Next morning, Betsy called while Augusta was out. She was very much looking forward to having Mrs. Dabney, Augusta and Adam to lunch at one o'clock.

"I told her I wasn't perfectly certain about you," Mrs. Dabney said. "I know you often like to read while Adam naps rather than go gallivanting out to lunch."

"I certainly won't go if you've told her I'm not coming." Augusta plunked bags of groceries on the counter.

"Honey, I only told her I wasn't certain."

"Well, now you are."

"Augusta, won't you come? We could stay just a short time, and bring Adam back in time for his nap."

"Thank you, I'd rather stay here and eat a peanut-butter sandwich. And you'll enjoy yourself much more without me."

With a small sigh, Mrs. Dabney turned away.

When speculating about parenthood, Augusta had sometimes thought that an interesting aspect of the biological difference between men and women was the fact that a woman could not fail to know she had conceived a child, and that it was hers, her own flesh and blood and bone; she need not necessarily know who had fathered the child, and even if she aborted it the conception of that child would be forever a vital part of her experience. Whereas a man was capable of fathering countless children and remaining ignorant of the existence of any of them. Augusta did not find it impossible to believe that Tom was Betsy's father. Rather, she did not want to believe it. She deeply resented her mother's having endowed Desert Gap with a Nashville past. Desert Gap was Augusta's town, and she had intended to share it with her mother. Instead, her mother was sharing with Augusta what she knew about the town, and had been doing so for three weeks. She had established connections all up and down the alphabetized streets and numbered avenues, and had made her usual cosy circle out of Augusta's brave new world. Abe Gottlieb had cousins in Shelbyville, the sister of someone on K Street had been in Augusta's class at Vassar, someone's uncle taught chemistry at Sewanee where Augusta's cousin was a student, another person's parents were the "delightful Chicagoans" whom Augusta's parents had met while going by boat from Padua to Venice. And now — *such* a small world — the man down the street was, all unawares, the father of a woman up the street to whose mother Augusta's great-uncle had been godfather. Or so Mrs. Dabney would have it.

She and Betsy had had a right good time, Mrs. Dabney reported. Betsy had made a perfectly delicious avocado mousse and had been kind enough to give her the recipe for it.

"And in exchange, did you tell her who her daddy is?"

Mrs. Dabney untied her striped silk scarf, laid it neatly on top of her handbag, and turned to face Augusta. "You're angry with me, aren't you, because I told you about Tom Patterson. I'm sorry about that, I hadn't realized it would upset you so. It's been on my mind ever since I saw him, there on his lawn picking up my postcards. And then Betsy Perkins told me she'd been born Betsy Todd, and he walked into the room while she was sitting there! Why, it was like a play. It was all I could do not to introduce them to each other."

"Wouldn't that have been a dramatic moment. The second-act curtain drops, we all go out for drinks and wonder what happens in the third act."

"Of course I would never have done it. But I couldn't keep from telling my own daughter, could I? It was all told to me when I wasn't much younger than you. I suppose you'll say things like this happen all the time and no doubt they do, statistically speaking. But when you know the people involved they can't be statistics, can they. You do a lot of remembering about them, and you find out to your surprise that they're a part of your own life, all bound up with your other memories. Because what is life, really, what do you think about, looking back, except the people who've slipped in and out of your life? And sometimes those you've known the least have left the strongest impression. I didn't know Tom at all well. Chiefly I knew about him. And the only time I ever saw Betsy she was being a flower-girl in a wedding — by then I knew her story so I was particularly interested in her. She wasn't a pretty little girl, but she had her mother's only good feature — the eyes. It was shortly after Sue was born so I knew how a mother felt about her child, and I kept thinking about Betsy's poor mother, whose life was so tragic. Though you might think tragic too strong a word for what is perhaps quite an ordinary little story."

"Adam should be outside. Why don't we sit out there?" Augusta was too stubborn to say outright that she wanted to hear the ordinary little story.

"Do you remember," her mother began, when they were seated on the patio and Adam was bouncing in his swing, "the old white house with the stone verandah and the big square tower, just up the lane from Uncle Rennie's house? You used to say it was haunted —— "

Augusta interrupted. "To children, all deserted old houses are haunted." She intended to be disparaging, but memory took over in spite of herself, and she went on in a different tone. "Besides, somebody did tell us — the Peytons and Betty Jean and me. We used to play there, and an old Negro with a wooden leg told us about the ghost. I guess he thought he'd scare us away. Was he a kind of caretaker? He used to turn up and putter around with a rake. Not that there was anything to rake — the whole place was a thicket of thorns and briars. And hundreds of rabbits...." Sleeping Beauty's Castle, they had called it. It gave her a kind of thrill, now, to think of children being allowed to run as wild and free as they had: building secret hideaways in rickety lofts and stables, daring each other to crawl through culverts in which they might be wedged fast for ever, to die in the darkness with rats gnawing on them. There was a crumbling high brick wall they had climbed, into an overgrown garden belonging to a person they believed to be a witch, to steal wormy pears and the raspberries that hung in velvet clusters on the canes. It had taken great daring because they knew that if she caught them she would give them the evil eye and they would turn to stone. And best of all, those excursions to the abandoned house at the end of the long lane that ran through bosky woods. At the end of the lane stood the house, with paint peeling and shutters hanging from broken windows and the Bluebeard's tower. Around it grasses grew shoulder high, treacherous briars reached out and grabbed their legs and arms, tearing them. There was a grapevine so thick they could swing on it. They had easily found a way into the house through a broken cellar door, and explored echoing cobwebbed rooms bare of furniture, with bits of ceiling plaster on the floor, and broken glass. After the old man had told them about the ghost, they had sometimes seen a shadowy figure at the top of the staircase, or a wan, wild face at a window.

"... the old yard-boy," her mother was saying. "He'd worked there for many years, he'd have had a proprietary interest in the place. It's gone now. There's a retirement home in its place. At any rate, that's where Betsy Todd was born. Her mother was Lucy Montgomery, the only child of Colonel Montgomery. I don't remember Mrs. Montgomery. She died when Lucy was a little girl. My mother said of her that she was a poor timid thing and that her spirit had been crushed by her husband. He was a ramrod of a man, with a disagreeable manner. Lucy was in my class at Miss Templeton's and we were unkind to her, I'm sorry to say. It's shameful to remember the unkindness of which you were capable, as a child. Lucy was knobby-looking, with pale thin hair. When she was called upon to recite in class, or even when she was spoken to, she jumped, as if somebody had poked her, and blushed. Violently, not prettily. She was extremely intelligent — no doubt we resented that — and she was always pathetically eager to help any of us in our schoolwork. We accepted her help, but we didn't accept her." She glanced at Augusta. "Yes, I know it was cruel. Lucy was sickly, and was often out of school for days at a time, but even so she was always head of the class. But never a teacher's pet. Poor Lucy. All she had in her favour was a pair of pretty eyes."

"She had intelligence, too. If she hadn't been brought up in a cluster of southern belles she'd probably have made something of herself."

"I think you're quite right about that. There wasn't much future for girls in those days, beyond marriage. Which was all most of us wanted. I admit we were a frivolous lot. Of that I'm not ashamed, as I am of the unkindness. I think there's a time for frivolity and fun and dancing, and I look back on those years with pleasure. But Lucy must have suffered at those parties and dances. She was too shy to get around her plainness with bright talk and flirting."

"Or too intelligent."

"Or too intelligent, as you say. Her father brought her to dances and then came back to take her home. Sometimes a particularly kind boy would dance with her. Mostly she sat in the dressing-room or bedroom or wherever the girls were gathering between dances to powder their noses and so on. Sometimes she even brought a book with her."

"Bully for her! I like her."

Mrs. Dabney smiled. "You know, Augusta, you make me like her too. Well — somehow she got herself a beau. It caused quite a stir, Lucy arriving at the New Year's Eve cotillion not with her father but with a young man. Tall and handsome, perfectly well turned out but...he was a caddy at the golf club. I know, I know" — she held up a hand as if it were a flag of truce — "it is contemptible, having to admit that, but it is all part of the story of those days. So when he beaued Lucy around there were those who made derogatory remarks, all of which you can easily imagine. If he hadn't been an outsider it would have been different. But he wasn't one of us in any way. He came from somewhere up north, he caddied to earn extra money, and he waited on table at Vanderbilt. . . ."

Augusta was staring at her mother as a judge might stare at a petty criminal defending himself.

". . . remember, I'm not proud to be telling you this. Merely painting the whole picture. I don't think I ever outright snubbed him. For one thing he never did ask me to dance. Chiefly I remember that I was struck — as others were — by his resemblance to Curtiss Dabney. I played up to Curtiss Dabney because he was cousin to John Dabney who was two years older and who in my opinion had hung the moon. I am still of that opinion."

Augusta disregarded that. "What was the embarrassing incident about Curtiss?"

"A trifle. A pretty girl named Mary-Brett ran up behind Tom Patterson and clapped her hands over his eyes and said, 'Guess who?' Of course he couldn't guess and Mary-Brett was perfectly mortified over her mistake and said, 'Why, you're not Curtiss! You're an impostor!' Poor Lucy was standing there. She went red as that geranium."

Augusta drew her breath in sharply. "God, I'm glad I didn't grow up in Nashville in your day! It was even worse than mine. At least a few of us were beginning to be conscious. I should think you'd be glad Tom doesn't remember you. Maybe he does, maybe he remembers the cruelty."

"I regret it. I wanted, in some way, to tell him that."

"It's a little late." She picked Adam up and sat down with him in her arms. He was content for a moment then, rebellious, wriggled free. She put him down on the brick floor in a circle of toys, and looked at her mother.

"So...we saw them on and off for about five months, and just as we'd all got used to Lucy having a beau, she hadn't a beau any longer. But then a good many of us hadn't. We were at war with Germany by then and all the fine young men had joined up. Some — like John Dabney who was at Princeton — hadn't even waited to graduate. All at once everyone was in uniform and for a little while life seemed gayer than ever and when we weren't kicking up our heels or thinking about love and laughter and bravery and courage we were rolling bandages for the Red Cross or making up boxes of cookies for the boys in camp. Lucy didn't join in any of this. Tom had gone off to war, but Lucy had disappeared too. We heard she was sick again and confined to her room and I'm afraid we didn't pay much attention. It was the more shocking then to hear shortly after Thanksgiving that Lucy Montgomery was dead. The funeral was private, which in those days was unusual. It all seemed very strange and terrible, and we talked about it in hushed voices and couldn't believe it had happened. It was the first death in our circle, but the news of it was overshadowed by news of all the American boys being killed overseas and two days later a Nashville boy we all adored was killed in France and that took our minds off poor Lucy."

"What did she die of?" Augusta asked.

"Of a weak heart, it was said. But it was of Betsy she died, and of a broken heart."

As a child Augusta had been both horrified and fascinated by stories in which people died of a "broken heart", picturing a heart jaggedly cracked in two and bleeding. Even now the words had a disagreeable effect on her. "How do you know? If it were really true and *you* knew it, hundreds of other people would know it."

"I knew it," Mrs. Dabney said, "because it was Uncle Rennie who delivered the baby and arranged for the adoption. It was all done in the greatest secrecy."

"Then how do you know?" Augusta persisted. "Physicians are supposed to keep professional secrets. I'm surprised at Uncle Rennie, blabbing about it. It was unethical."

"Reynolds Tucker was the most honourable man in the world." Mrs. Dabney spoke with composure. "And Aunt Charlotte the most honourable woman. She and my mother were closer as sisters-in-law than any sisters I've ever known. My mother was always her confidante. Even in those days it was unusual for a doctor's wife to be handed a new-born to take care of. That's what happened. Uncle Rennie brought the baby home to her and of course he told her whose it was. They trusted each other. But the Todds, who were longing for a baby, never were told whose child they'd adopted." She paused, reflecting. "I've always thought that my mother, in telling me about Lucy — I've no idea now how the subject came up, I remember only that it was shortly after Sue was born — meant me to know that I was a grown woman now, no longer a giddy girl from whom terrible tales must be kept. I heard the whole story: how Uncle Rennie was roused up in the middle of the night to go to the Colonel's, and how right up to the time he showed the Colonel the baby girl wrapped up in a blanket, the Colonel pretended not to know what ailed his daughter. . . . "

"He must have been insane. Anywhere else he'd have been locked up."

"Nowadays, I expect they'd have a word for what ailed him. He wouldn't even look at the baby. 'Take it out of my sight,' he said, 'I'll have nothing to do with it.' Uncle Rennie took the baby back to the bedroom and he sat with Lucy doing what he could to comfort her until she died, which she shortly did. He thought of fetching Lucy's father, then he thought, No, let her die in peace. She'd suffered terribly. It was a breech birth. He said she might have been in labour for two days. Poor Lucy, she was too unhappy to live, let alone to give birth."

"Why would the old monster send for a doctor? Why would he risk having a stranger around?"

"It would have been more peculiar if he hadn't called a doctor. No doubt he was desperate, fearing she'd never give birth and her agony would go on in his house for ever. And then he knew he could trust Reynolds Tucker, who was as humane as he was scrupulous, and would take care of everything including Lucy's reputation, whatever happened. Can you imagine, he tried to *pay* Uncle Rennie. It was only for the sake of the baby that Uncle Rennie didn't walk out of the house there and then. He did a clever thing: before he signed the death certificate saying that Lucy had died of heart failure — which in a way she did, her heart simply gave out — he extracted a promise from the Colonel that he would never under any circumstance attempt to trace the baby. Not that he would have, I'm certain. Still, Uncle Rennie swore the Colonel to secrecy and then he had the upper hand. Lucy's name could rest quietly along with her, and his god-daughter Julia Todd could have the baby she'd been longing for. You could do such things in those days, before the government tied everything up in red tape and people learned not to trust each other. And Hester, the good old mammy who'd brought all of us up, took care of the 'foundling' and in a few days the Todds came on from Savannah and they loved the baby on sight, and straight off named her Elizabeth — Betsy for short — and carried her back with them. I'm the only living person who knows who Betsy Perkins is. Except that now you know too."

"I wish I didn't! It's too dreadful. Don't you see, that's what I loathe about the South. It's full of stories like that, it feeds on them."

"Any place has stories like that. Any place that's been there long enough to have human beings live in it. Some day Desert Gap will have its stories too."

"It has one now. You've just told it."

"But don't you find it even a little intriguing?" Mrs. Dabney's tone brightened, as she returned to the present. "That I, knowing all about this but having no reason for years and years to think about it, should find Betsy Todd out here being your friend and neighbour? And her father, too, just a few doors away? I never heard that Tom Patterson returned to Nashville and I thought that perhaps, in the heartless way some men have, he might never have given a thought to the girl he'd courted, never wondered if anything had come of their passion. But he married so late in life. It makes me wonder if he ever did go back to find her? Perhaps he did, perhaps he visited her grave...."

"Now you're fabricating. I believe all you say about Betsy Perkins and who she is, but about Tom you really haven't a shred of evidence. He took Lucy to some dances. Does that make him the father of her child? Or did Lucy whisper to Uncle Rennie, on her dying breath, 'Tom Patterson is the father of my child'?" Immediately, she regretted having said that, having poked fun at Lucy Montgomery as her mother and her mother's friends had done in their cruel years.

Mrs. Dabney was magnanimous enough to ignore the gibe. "You don't need proof for everything you know about people. Birth and marriage and death certificates, all the cards people carry, only tell you statistics. They don't tell you anything about the people themselves." She touched Augusta's hand. "Do look at your son, sniffing so appreciatively at the rose geranium he's plucked. How I wish your father were here, with his camera."

When Adam had been bathed and fed and put to bed and sung to by his grandmother, Augusta made drinks and carried them out to the patio. "You're sure it's not too chilly for you?"

"No, the air is delicious. It's only the damp I mind." Mrs. Dabney was knitting a sweater for Adam. The metal needles clicked rhythmically, glinting in and out of the cherry-red wool. Beside her, the lemon tree stood in its redwood tub, its seventeen lemons hanging like decorations among the dark, shining leaves.

Sipping at her drink, Augusta smelled the mint sprig

she had stuck in it. The mint had flourished too, like everything else her mother had planted. Mrs. Dabney put down her knitting, picked up her glass. "To your good health, honey."

For an instant Augusta had the sensation, perhaps induced by the smell of mint, that the two of them were sitting on the wisteria-hung verandah in Nashville, waiting while shadows deepened across the lawn for her father to come home to dinner, home to a glass of bourbon with mint in it, home to the house he had been born in. She saw it all with extraordinary clarity — the shadowed lawn, the summer-house at the bottom of the garden, the tulip tree, the flowers softly burning in the twilight. It was uncanny, as though it were a photograph that had superimposed itself on another photograph of a backyard patio, behind which hung the desert sky and the mountains. Then it slipped away again, and she was looking across the small yard and over the bamboo fence at the flat roof of the house opposite them on Q Street, and at the sky transparent in its clarity and pierced in the distance by jagged peaks that had caught fire from the sun dropping behind them. As she watched, the fires burned out. Until the stars came out, and the moon rose, there would be nothing at all to shelter the earth. There was nothing now but space.

"I'll have this sweater done before I leave tomorrow." Mrs. Dabney held it up for Augusta's inspection. "How the time has flown." She drank a little bourbon, put the glass down and took up her knitting again. "By the way, I think Betsy would be pleased to have some of your mint. She hadn't realized it could be grown here. In a few months you should have plenty to give away, if you'd be so kind. Be sure to remind her that she must put it by a dripping faucet where it can drink all it wants until it gets well rooted."

Augusta had a mind to say that on the desert you could not have faucets dripping day and night while mint rooted itself. Didn't her mother realize that water was precious, on the desert? Instead, she said, "Abe Gottlieb wants some of your mint, too." She pictured mint growing in Betsy's garden, and Abe's, and then in other gardens. Soon Desert Gap would be one big patch of southern mint. And by the same token, when her mother went back to Nashville she would make Desert Gap sound like a small southern town.

Augusta turned to look at her, apprehensive. "What are you going to do with this tale you've unearthed? Are you going to call up your friends and tell them about this amazing coincidence?"

Mrs. Dabney gave her a look — an authoritative look of the kind Augusta had not had from her in a long time. "What do you take me for? I spoke of it to you because you are my daughter. Just as my mother spoke of it to me. It would not occur to me to make gossip of it. To do so would be unthinkable. Not to say extremely dangerous, tampering with other people's lives."

Augusta muttered, "Sorry."

"Not at all." Mrs. Dabney's voice was polite, rather cool.

After a moment Augusta said, "What worries me . . . ." She stopped, frowning. Then burst out, "What am I going to do, knowing? How can I be with Betsy, and not think of that harrowing tale? Or with Tom? Don't you see it changes everything?"

"It doesn't change them."

"It does, for me. Inside." She could feel the secret beating away inside her, already a part of her.

"Augusta dear, when you're as old as I am you'll know lots of secrets too. At least, I hope you will. Your life won't have been very rich if you go to your grave without any secrets locked away in your heart."

A quality in her tone, a fullness in it, caught Augusta's attention. They exchanged a look, for the first time not as mother and daughter but as women, and Augusta found herself drawn willy-nilly out of her world of the future into a world that had existed for ever, a world to which Desert Gap had from the start belonged. She was aware that she would always know, as she knew now, that wherever she went, to an ancient town or a new one, she would find that the past had been there ahead of her, leaving its secrets behind.